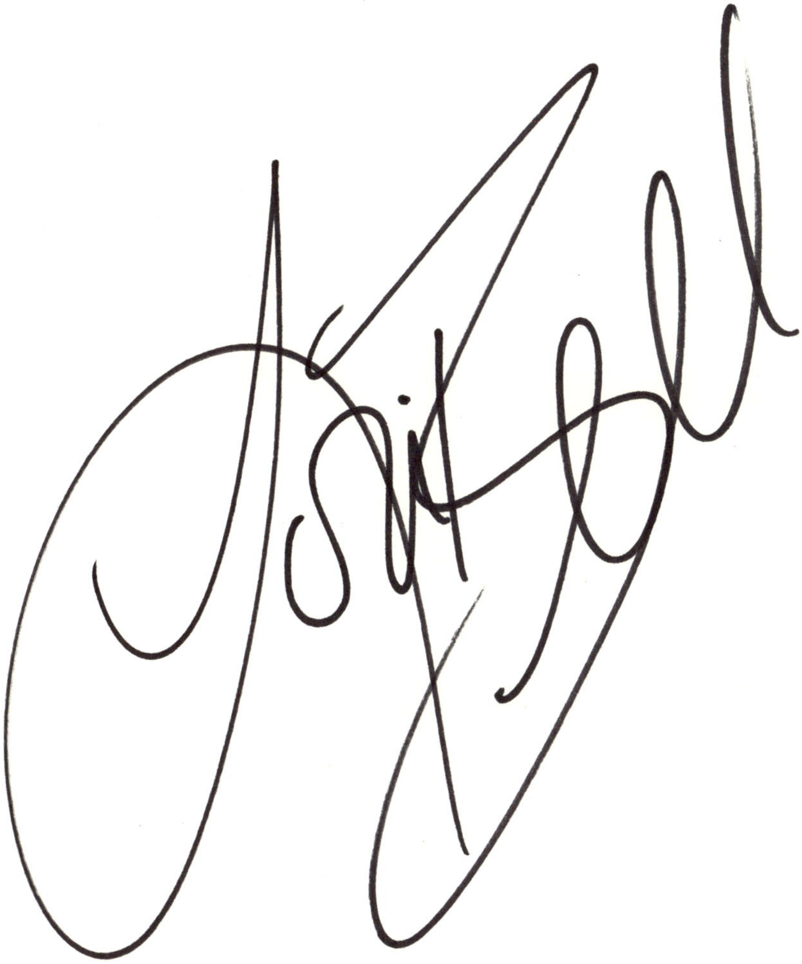

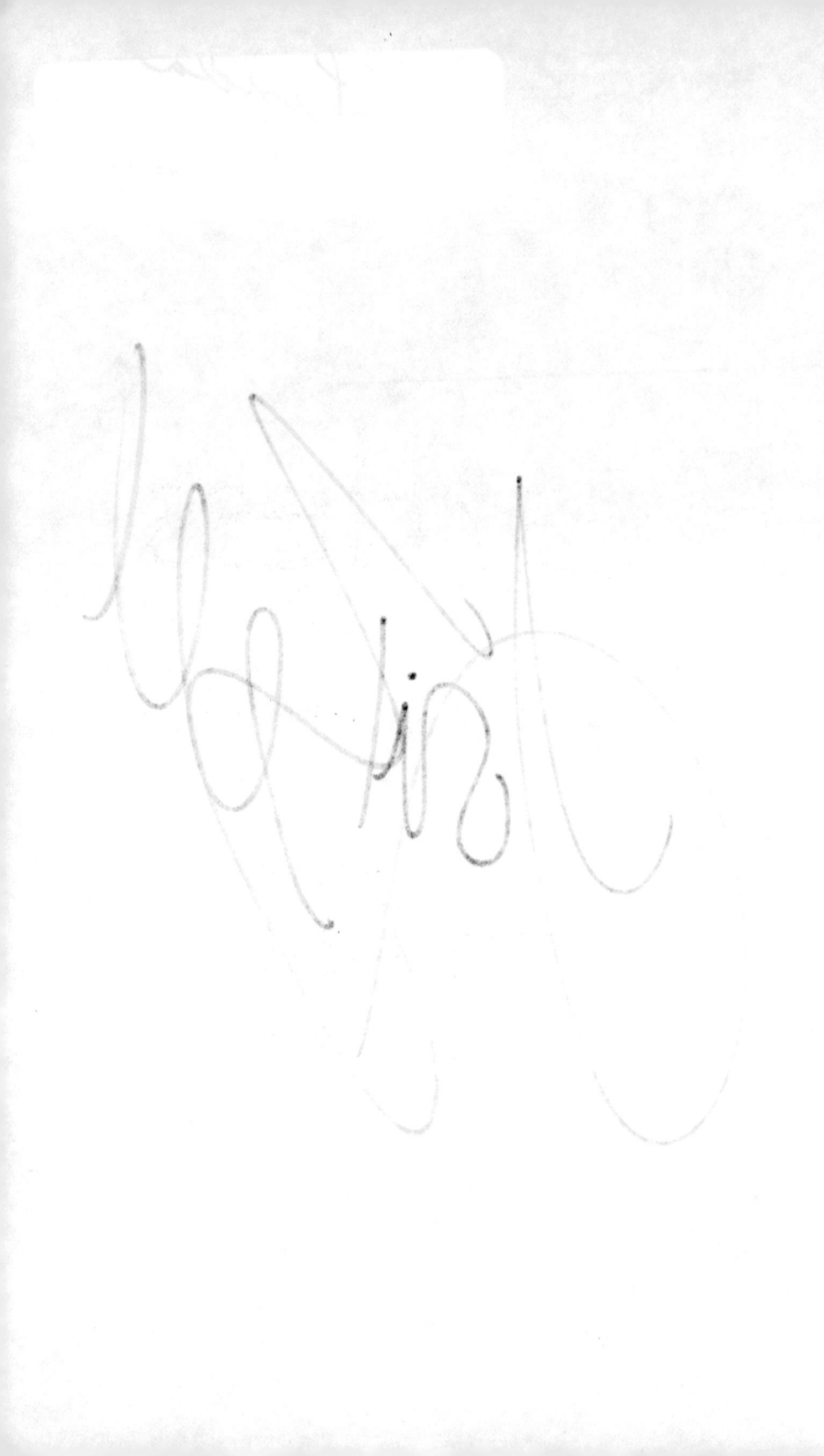

Heartless

Lori Bell

This book is a work of fiction. Names, characters, places and incidents are the product of the author's imagination or are used fictitiously. Any resemblance to actual events, locales, or persons, living or dead, is coincidental.

Copyright © 2015 by Lori Bell

All rights reserved. This book or any portion thereof may not be reproduced or used in any manner whatsoever without the express written permission of the publisher except for the use of brief quotations in a book review.

Cover photograph by Angie Evans

http://en.wikipedia.org/wiki/Emphysema#P...
http://www.nlm.nih.gov/medlineplus/ency/...
http://www.merck.com/mmpe/sec05/ch049/ch...
http://www.merck.com/mmpe/sec05/ch049/ch...
 http://www.livestrong.com/article/521880-can-taking-baby-aspirin-help-with-a-pregnancy/Conception
http://www.webmd.com/diabetes/tc/type-2-diabetes-in-children-medications
http://en.wikipedia.org/wiki/Amniotic_fluid_embolism

Printed by CreateSpace

ISBN 978-1507610695

DEDICATION

This book is dedicated to all of my incredible readers. Without you, I would not have been inspired to write four books in one year! Your encouragement is immeasurable to me.

Chapter 1

She pulled up in her old, gray Jeep Cherokee as close to the beach as she could get. Living in a house right on the sand and near the ocean water seemed like a good idea at the time. Kerrigan Ross just wanted to be alone for the summer. She needed time to think. And to heal. Hopefully, to heal.

As she walked, carrying her suitcase in one hand and a Diet Coke in the other, the flip flops on her feet felt heavy in the sand so she stepped out of them and tried to free one hand to pick them up. When she set her soda can down, pushing it hard into the sand to force it to remain upright, it tipped over and spilled. The beautiful white sand of Orange Beach, Alabama was flooded with dark brown liquid near Kerrigan's bare feet. *Leave it to me*, she thought, *anything beautiful in my life always turns ugly.*

Heartless

She left the soda spill fizzing in the hot sand and continued to walk until she reached the weathered, wooden deck leading up to the last beach house. There were three houses, all in a row, side by side. The houses weren't fancy, all three had powder blue siding and pale yellow shutters, but there was something vintage about the way they looked and Kerrigan felt a small sense of belonging as she put her flip flops back on and stepped up onto the deck.

She reached the door, set her suitcase down at her feet, and then bent down to fold back the mat where a house key lay hidden underneath. Not too original, but Kerrigan's friend, Macie Jane, assured her the beach house community is a quiet and safe one. Kerrigan held the silver key close to her mouth and blew the sand off of it before she inserted it into the keyhole, turned it, and unlocked what would be her home for the next four months.

The house looked cozy to Kerrigan as she stepped inside, closing the door behind her. The old wooden flooring had long lost its shine all throughout the place. There were two multi-colored, sizeable area rugs in the living room and bedroom, and large, square, cream-colored tile flooring in the tiny bathroom. Macie Jane had kept the place clean and adequately decorated. Nothing was overly fancy, but all of the furniture and even the appliances in the kitchen looked modern and in good condition.

After walking through the house and leaving her suitcase in the bedroom, Kerrigan went into the kitchen and opened the refrigerator door. She had not eaten since yesterday. The one-thousand-mile drive from Baltimore,

Maryland to Orange Beach, Alabama had taken her almost seventeen hours with only a few stops to refill the gas tank in her old jeep. Each time she stopped, she bought more Diet Coke for the road.

She smiled to herself when she looked into the refrigerator and saw a case of Diet Coke on the bottom shelf with a post-it note attached to it. *I know you live on this stuff. Make yourself at home.* Macie Jane was Kerrigan's roommate in college and the two of them have remained present in each other's lives since graduation six years ago.

Kerrigan closed the refrigerator door and walked back into the bedroom to retrieve her cell phone from inside of her suitcase. She had turned it off when she left the previous evening and never once wanted to power it back on. The long, quiet drive all night long allowed her to do a lot of thinking, maybe too much. But, she knew this beach house was the right place for her to be right now.

When she powered on the phone, she noticed the missed calls and then she purposely deleted the unread text messages. She found her contact list and selected MJ's name. Macie Jane's closest friends call her MJ and despite the distance in miles between the two women, they could always count on each other. Kerrigan sent MJ a short text, *I've arrived. The place looks great. Thank you for offering it to me rent-free all summer! You know I need this.* She turned off her phone again and opened the chest of drawers near the window and placed her phone inside the empty top drawer and closed it. She would unpack her suitcase later. Right now she just wanted to stretch her legs some more, maybe even walk the beach. The afternoon sunny skies and eighty degrees felt perfect for early May. Still wearing her black flip flops with black athletic shorts and an oversized emerald-green t-shirt with the letters EMT written on the front in white block letters, Kerrigan was already dressed comfortably to be outside. She may have had comfortable clothes on, but it had been a long time since she felt comfortable in her own skin. Kerrigan fell into the category of being overweight. In college, she thought a size ten made her look and feel fat. Now at twenty-eight years old, she is thirty-five pounds heavier and feeling it. She wished she could again squeeze into a ten.

She had her long, naturally curly, dark brown hair pulled up into a knot on top of her head where her sunglasses were too. All set to take a walk as she grabbed the house key off of the kitchen counter and walked out. She locked the door and then placed the key under the mat again before she walked the length of the deck leading out to the beach.

As she was about to step off the end of the deck, she spotted a heavy-set, elderly woman, wearing a lime green muu-muu dress and sandy brown Birkenstock sandals, waddling a little as she walked in the sand and stepped up onto the deck near Kerrigan. "Hi, welcome! Macie Jane told me to expect you. She paid me for the summer's rent already, so I won't be hassling you, honey. I own all three of these little beach houses and it would be a bitch if my renters didn't follow through with their share, ya know?" Thirty seconds ago, Kerrigan had absolutely no idea who this short, stocky, snow-white-haired woman walking toward her was.

But, now, after her non-stop winded talking, Kerrigan already knew she was the beach-housing landlord. *MJ must have forgotten to warn me of this one*, she thought, as she watched the woman help herself to a lounge chair on the deck. "Sorry honey, I gotta sit down. I'm out of air. My shitty excuse for lungs just do not get me very far these days, especially when I've been walking and talking."

So much for my walk, Kerrigan thought. She still had not spoken a single word to this woman. She, in part, did not let her get a word in, but Kerrigan had not come here to socialize. Or to make friends.

"Don't just stand there honey, sit down with me, tell me about yourself." The last thing Kerrigan wanted was to get into her life story with a stranger, but given the fact that this woman owned the place she would be living in all summer, she knew she had to be polite. Kerrigan sat down in the other lounge chair next to her new neighbor, the landlady.

"I think I'd rather hear about you," Kerrigan said, feeling like she could have rolled her eyes back into her head. "It must be interesting living on the beach. How long have you been here?"

"I've been here since my husband died twenty-one years ago. I needed a change, so I sold our home in Mobile and bought these three beauties here on the beach." As the landlady was talking, Kerrigan noticed the bronze color of her skin. She obviously loved the sun, and Kerrigan suddenly felt self-conscious knowing she looked pasty in May. She intended to change that this summer. What else did she have to do but soak up the rays? "How about you, what brings you to Alabama? When Macie Jane told me she would be gone for the summer, all she said is her friend from Baltimore is going to hold down the fort."

"A getaway, I guess you could say," Kerrigan answered, vaguely.

"Well, anytime you need anything, you just holler, okay? Did I tell you my name is Hallie?" Kerrigan shook her head no, and said, "I'm Kerrigan."

"What kind of name is Kerrigan anyway?" Hallie asked, obviously showing no couth.

"My birth name, I was told it was my mother's maiden name," Kerrigan explained. "I never knew my biological parents. I was put up for adoption immediately after I was born. A name was all they left with me."

"Oh my," Hallie said, "I sure hope someone snatched you up right away. You know, there are so many people out there who cannot have babies or something ends up being wrong. It's just a blessing when a baby is born healthy. What I'm getting at is, we didn't have to worry as much years ago as we do now – about everything!" Kerrigan drifted off in thought, as Hallie continued to ramble, and she turned away and stared out at the ocean water.

Then, suddenly, Kerrigan stood up from her chair and spoke as she walked away. "I think I'm going to go for a walk now." Kerrigan left Hallie sitting alone on the deck outside of the house she was going to call home all summer long. She began hoping her quest to find some peace and quiet would be feasible here.

***

It was dark outside by the time Kerrigan made her way back to the bedroom of the beach house to unpack her suitcase. She had spent hours outside today, walking the beach and sitting on the deck. She also made a trip into town to buy a few groceries, but all she had felt like eating was a bowl of cereal and drinking two more Diet Cokes. She had not seen Hallie again since this afternoon, but she did notice light in her middle beach house tonight. She hadn't seen anyone come and go from the first beach house, the one located on the other side of Hallie's, but whoever was living on the beach near her this summer really didn't concern Kerrigan. She was there to feel the sun on her face as she had today, and she felt a little better because of it.

She stood at the foot of the bed, it was a sleigh bed with light oak wood. It looked like something that belonged inside of a log cabin, not a beach house. She smiled to herself, thinking of MJ. *That is just like her. If you like something, who cares if it doesn't go? Think outside of the box. Be different. To hell with what should or shouldn't be.* Kerrigan wished she could develop a mindset like that. Maybe now, she had. She did pick up instantaneously to end up here.

When she unzipped the suitcase, she took out all of her clothes and put them into the empty dresser drawers. She didn't have anything to hang in the closet. She had packed light, just her summer clothes, which were mainly comfortable, elastic shorts and oversized t-shirts, and one swimsuit which she doubted would still fit her. It didn't take her long to unpack her clothes and put her hairdryer and toiletries in the bathroom. There was only one bathroom in the beach house and it was located in the hallway, catty-cornered from the bedroom. When she returned to her suitcase, she unzipped the outside pocket last. She thought about leaving it in there, but she wanted to feel it in her hands and bring it up to her face. She inhaled. The small, yellow thermal blanket with silk-trim on all four sides still kept the scent Kerrigan hoped would never fade.

Three weeks ago

Chapter 2

Kerrigan woke up with a start. Her husband, Keith, was asleep beside her. She sat up abruptly, focusing on the clock on the nightstand alongside the bed. It was five o'clock in the morning, five hours since the baby's last feeding. Piper Rose, at five weeks old, has yet to sleep more than two and a half consecutive hours a night. *Maybe she is moving out of the phase most newborns go through,* Kerrigan thought, but she couldn't shake the feeling she was having. She felt chilled as she got out of bed, grabbed her white fleece robe off of the hook on the closet door, and moved quietly, but quickly, into her baby girl's nursery.

Her baby no longer fit inside of the bassinet beside their bed, and she had been in her crib for an entire week already. Kerrigan had questioned putting the baby in her own room so soon. She wanted to see and hear her every move. But, Keith reassured her how *she will be just fine. She may even sleep better, longer between feedings, if she has room to stretch out in her crib.* Kerrigan remembered her husband's words and began to calm down as she approached the crib to look at her sleeping baby girl.

What she found when she peeked into the crib was devastating, shocking, sickening, and so utterly final. Piper Rose looked like a statue, something hard or frozen. And this moment will be frozen in Kerrigan's memory for the rest of her life.

She immediately picked up her baby, noticing she had been lying face down, as she screamed hysterically for Keith to wake up. "Keith! No! Oh my God, Keith! Get in here!" When Keith came rushing to the doorway of the baby's nursery, he stopped himself with both of his hands on the door frame as he witnessed his wife on her knees on the carpet in front of the crib, attempting CPR on their baby girl. He didn't move, standing there wearing only his navy blue and white checkered boxer shorts, as she worked on their baby, crying and struggling to talk in between breaths of life which she was trying so very desperately to pump into their baby girl. "It's been five hours since she was awake, she's not breathing, oh dear God help me!" Her plea was for God to help, she never asked Keith for his help. He, too, is an emergency medical technician like Kerrigan, but at this moment he could not remember anything, not a single life-saving procedure he was trained to perform. He's done it before. He's saved other adults, children, and even babies, but this time he could see his wife's efforts were useless. He knew it was too late. He had not even run out of the room to call 911. He and his wife are emergency responders and their baby's life was lost in their hands.

It had been too long, but Kerrigan refused to stop. She worked tirelessly on Piper Rose, crying hysterically and refusing to believe this awful truth. Her baby had died in the middle of the night with her being just right across the hallway. She had not heard her struggling to breathe, she was not there for her helpless baby. *What kind of mother am I?* Keith, a man just under six feet tall with a moderate beer gut, finally found the courage to step through the doorway and kneel down beside his wife. He wanted to touch their baby now. He just couldn't believe this was happening. He cried and he screamed and he stood up and threw the diaper genie pail against the wall as hard as he could before he fell back onto his knees with his face in his hands.

Kerrigan picked up her still baby girl off of the floor, *my God she felt like a hard, plastic doll,* as she swaddled her in a yellow blanket from inside of the crib and then she cradled her close in her arms. The tears were streaming down her cheeks, soaking her face, as she looked over at her husband, now standing in the middle of the room with his thick, dark brown hair messy on his head, slumped shoulders, and teary, red eyes. "How did this happen to her, Keith?" Kerrigan choked on her words, but he understood her. "I put her down after you fed her. We talked about this, Kerri." His voice was shaking as his wife glared at him with the baby that was lost to them, still in her arms.

"Tell me you placed her down in her crib on her back," Kerrigan's words were firm and cold toward him because she already knew what his answer was going to be. They had been concerned about the flat area forming on the back of Piper's head from sleeping on her back. They had tried more tummy time during the day, but Piper always fussed in that position. In the nursery, they have a side sleeper which is designed to place a baby on its side while sleeping. The cushions, held in placed by Velcro fabric strips, were supposed to keep babies in position while sleeping. Kerrigan was not ready to use the side sleeper yet, but Keith thought it was time to be concerned about their baby's soft scull flattening a little more each day. He didn't want their child *to have to wear a helmet, like the one they saw on that baby at the pediatrician's office the other day.* Kerrigan had brushed off his concerns as nothing. Their baby would be fine. Her soft little head would return to its normal shape once she grew bigger and stronger and would be on her back a little less each day. She looked into the crib again now and saw the side sleeper cushion right where she remembered it being in her state of panic. Either Keith had not tightened it properly, or Piper was already strong enough to move in her sleep. Whichever the case, Kerrigan had found her baby with her face down, muffled into one of the side sleeper's cushions, and she was the victim of Sudden Infant Death Syndrome.

Keith didn't answer with words, but the regret in his eyes, the sorrow and the guilt on his face, told Kerrigan exactly what had happened, what her husband had done.

She wanted to tear him apart. She wanted to reverse time, just five hours, just five fucking hours, to make this be untrue.

"You did this to her, you son of a bitch." Kerrigan's words were barely a whisper, but Keith had heard every single one, and the pain piercing his body, mind and soul right now was unbearable. He walked out of the room in sobs as he went to call an ambulance. There was no emergency. Not any longer. His baby was gone. And his wife blamed him.

***

When the ambulance pulled up to their small, modest home in Baltimore, there were no lights or sirens. The two paramedics were friends and co-workers of both Kerrigan and Keith, and their hearts were breaking for what they had heard happened and for what they were about to do.

Kerrigan did not look up from her rocking chair, she just continued to rock Piper and to hum. Keith walked into the room first as Erin and Chad followed. And when Keith told Kerrigan they came to take Piper, she ignored him. All four of them have seen instances like this before. Emergencies, grief, loss often sent people into shock or denial. It was always extremely sad to see, but this time it was too personal and overwhelmingly heart-wrenching for all of them. Erin could not bring herself to do it. She backed out of the nursery, crying.

Forty-five minutes passed in that nursery. Kerrigan would not listen. She would not give up her baby. Finally, he did not want to do it, but Keith held Kerrigan down in the rocking chair with every ounce of strength he had inside of him as Chad took the baby from her arms. "No!" Kerrigan screamed. "No, No, No! I won't let you take her. Please! Not like this. Don't force me. I need more time to say goodbye to her." Both men could not take this scene anymore. Especially, Keith. He was Piper's father, but he could not do it. He could not say goodbye to his lifeless baby. He left Kerrigan alone in the nursery, once again holding their baby girl who was already gone from this world. He would remember the feel of her little hand wrapped around his finger for the rest of his life. The chances were lost to experience anything else with his little girl, and when he reached the living room he fell apart with Erin and Chad both attempting to hold him up and console him.

Kerrigan could hear her husband's emotional breakdown, but she blocked out his pain as she laid her baby down on her crib mattress one last time. She placed her on her back, and she pulled the little yellow blanket away from the white sleeper with pink flowers on it. She dressed her in it last night after her bath. There would not be another bath. She would not wear all of the other sleepers and little items of clothing hanging in her small closet, ready and waiting for her to grow. Kerrigan was robbed of this chance to be Piper's mommy, and she had never known a feeling more crippling. She thought having a miscarriage had taken her heart, and it had for quite some time, but having carried Piper inside of her for nine months and then seeing and knowing her as real, and touching her, and taking care of her, and loving her had completed Kerrigan. And now this happened. How cruel. And how in the world was she expected to ever survive this unimaginable loss?

Her strength momentarily came from out of nowhere as Kerrigan unsnapped her baby's sleeper. She had to overstretch the material because her legs and arms would no longer bend. She blocked out that awful sight, that horrible feeling, as she removed the wet diaper from her baby and replaced it with a dry diaper on her bottom.

"There you go, my baby girl, now you are all fresh and clean again. Mommy wanted to take care of you like this forever." The tears broke loose as Kerrigan continued to struggle to dress her baby girl in that little white sleeper with pink flowers, one final time. "When you get to heaven, tell everyone who loves you up there to keep you safe for me, and to spoil you. It's not fair how they will get to hold you when I can't, but always know you're in my heart, Piper Rose. You *are* my heart."

***

The sight of her baby being placed into that tiny body bag, zipped closed, and carried out to the ambulance will stay with her forever. There should not even be such a thing for infants. It's wrong on so many levels. Just wrong. Maybe Kerrigan should not have remained in the room to watch. She has seen similar tragedies like this before, and again she was trained to handle it all. Those deaths, the deaths of young children, always affected Kerrigan in the worst way, but it was so different now, so unbelievably painful. This was happening to *her* now, and she vowed being an emergency medical technician and saving the lives of other people's loved ones was over for her. She no longer cared who needed help, or who lived or died, because her baby was gone.

 The funeral was like one of those horrific nightmares with sweating, shortness of breath, only to wake up and realize it's not real. In Kerrigan's case, it was real and her baby was laid out in a casket for family and friends to walk by, stare at, cry over, and then leave her with the same words. *I am so sorry for your loss. We are here if you need anything.* Those words fell on deaf ears. Kerrigan could not even bring herself to say *thank you* or mutter anything else to anyone. She returned hugs, she felt pangs of sympathy for others as they cried for her pain or because the story was just so sad. But, she could sense how frozen she was becoming inside, and she didn't know if she was capable of reversing that feeling.

 A fraction of Kerrigan's pain was familiar. Her miscarriage very early in her marriage had wreaked havoc on her heart. But, she gradually came out of that pain, and five years later Piper was born. Piper was her saving grace. And now there was no one left to save her.

 Keith desperately tried to reach out to her, and she listened when he spoke to her about blaming him for what everyone was calling SIDS. He told Kerrigan how he will always regret not placing their baby on her back that night, but he refused to believe it was solely his fault after they received the autopsy results. Piper Rose had an abnormality in the arcuate nucleus, which is the part of the brain that helps to control breathing and awakening during sleep. If a baby is breathing stale air and not getting enough oxygen, the brain usually triggers the baby to wake up and cry. The moment changes the breathing and heart rate, making up for the lack of oxygen. But a problem with the acruate nucleus could deprive the baby of this involuntary reaction. Kerrigan's medical background allowed her to fully understand this, but knowing it happened to her baby was inconceivable. Keith begged her to understand and not to place the blame on him. Her silence following Piper's death was chipping away at him, and their marriage.

***

Gail Boyd was sitting on the couch in Kerrigan and Keith's living room. She had been to their house every day since Piper's death. She was there every day regardless, as she and Kerrigan have been friends since they were eight years old. They have not shared a typical relationship between friends because many things have complicated their feelings for each other. But, when one of them was in need, the other was always there. This time, however, Gail's presence had not helped.

Gail kept pressuring Kerrigan to forgive her husband. Gail sided with Keith, reiterating to Kerrigan how this was not his fault. It unnerved Kerrigan to hear Gail stand up for a man who used to be hers. Keith and Gail were lovers in high school. Both of them were each other's first. Kerrigan had heard every detail of their relationship from Gail, but she always knew Keith would end up with a broken heart. And he did. When Gail moved away for college, she left him with the words, *I think we should see other people*.

And that is when Kerrigan unintentionally picked up the pieces. She and Keith had the same interests, and they both were studying to become paramedics. It took six months of hanging out, watching sports, riding four-wheelers together, and just being important in each other's lives before Keith saw Kerrigan as a woman, and not just one of the guys. She had a tomboy side to her and she meshed well with men, but she felt very much like a woman when she was with Keith.

When they became lovers, it seemed like the two of them were meant to be. Their relationship was comfortable, and easy. That is, until Gail found out it was happening. Gail had the long blonde hair, the better figure, and the piercing blue eyes with amazingly long eye lashes which she could bat once and have any man she desired. In anger, Gail warned Kerrigan that *her* story with Keith was not over. But, Kerrigan crushed any hope Gail had when she became pregnant with Keith's baby. And that was when Gail vowed to be a supportive friend to both of them, and to bury her feelings for Keith. She wanted to be a part of their lives with the baby.

Kerrigan and Keith were married for two months when she miscarried their baby at twelve weeks along. It was a heart-breaking time for the couple and Gail remained supportive. She had gotten used to the idea of them being married and sharing a life together, even if a baby no longer bonded them. Gail wanted the two of them to have more children, but when they lost Piper and she witnessed the pain Kerrigan was causing Keith, she saw that as cruel and unnecessary and she chose to be there for him.

It was three weeks after the baby's funeral. Kerrigan had not gone back to work, but Keith had. He needed to get out of the house. And when he was sitting on the couch next to Gail, he admitted how he went back to work to busy his mind and to distance himself from his wife. "I can't take this anymore," Keith said, as he sat beside Gail in the dim-lit living room. The television was off and only one lamp on the end table near the couch was on. Kerrigan had gone to bed almost an hour ago. She never wanted to be in the same room with Keith anymore. When he came home to find Gail in his house, he was relieved to have someone else to talk to there. Gail cooked dinner for the three of them and after they ate together, while mostly listening to Gail talk, Kerrigan retreated to her bedroom for the night. Keith helped Gail clean up the dishes before they sat down in the living room and began discussing Kerrigan.

"I think she needs professional help," Gail suggested. "She's so closed off, she's blaming you, she's going to lose it if we don't step in and force her to talk to someone." Gail was sitting close to Keith, as she always did because the woman knew no boundaries. She had her long blonde hair down in loose curls tonight and it reached well past her shoulders. She wore tight, black capri leggings and a long-sleeved fitted white t-shirt. Nothing fancy for a night spent at the home of her two closest friends, but Gail was aware she looked sexy. She was always aware of that. She had her shoes off and her feet were bare to show off her newly pedicured hot pink polished toes. Her legs were crossed as she faced Keith, sitting beside her.

"I know you're right, I just don't know when to bring it up to her," he said. "She is so fragile right now. I don't want to make things worse."

"I don't think we should wait, because she doesn't seem to be inching toward feeling any better, or coming out of this. I know it's going to take time, my God, she will never completely heal and neither will you," Gail said to Keith as she watched his eyes tear up. "Let's do this for her, together. I am here for you, baby. Always." She had not called him *baby* since their carefree years together in high school. He will never forget making love to her in the bed of his pick-up truck, under the stars. No woman since had ever made him feel the way Gail Boyd did. Not even his wife.

Keith didn't know if grief had consumed him, cluttered his thoughts, and stolen his sense of right and wrong, but at that moment he no longer cared. He put both of his hands on Gail's face and inched himself toward her. He met his lips with hers with no resistance as the two of them kissed and allowed a passion like no other to resurrect. Their lips touched, their tongues repeatedly intertwined, and when they finally pulled apart from each other, Keith spoke first with his hands still on her face. "You are so beautiful."

Kerrigan's husband had never said those exact words to her. He called her *sexy* when they were naked between the sheets and he wanted her. He may have even uttered the word *cute* a time or two when she attempted to get dolled up for him in her pre-pregnancy days. But, he had never called her *beautiful*. And he had never looked at her the way Kerrigan saw him look at Gail.

She was standing in the doorway of the kitchen, where she could see the back of the couch in the living room. She had come out of their bedroom to get a drink of water, when she noticed Gail still there, and she heard the two of them talking about suggesting a shrink. And then she watched him move closer to her and kiss her. Their kiss pained Kerrigan to stare at, but his words, her husband's words to her best friend, are what wounded her most. She had to get out of there.

Chapter 3

Kerrigan woke up at the beach house lying on top of her bedding. She had not even taken a shower, changed clothes, or crawled under the sheets last night. And she instantly remembered why. She was still holding the yellow baby blanket, and she had cried herself to sleep, yet again. It was just too much to bear. She could not handle knowing her baby was gone forever. She spent three weeks at home after Piper's death, crying and grieving and feeling so isolated from the rest of the world. Sure, people cared, called, and stopped by the house to check on her, but *their* lives went on. The rest of the world never stopped, but Kerrigan's world had come to an abrupt and terrifying halt.

Then, she left her husband. Yet another life-changing occurrence she had to force herself to get used to. It was Kerrigan's choice to leave, but after witnessing Keith and Gail betray her, she never wanted either one of them in her life, ever again. She now believed they deserved each other.

Kerrigan left the baby blanket on top of the bed's duvet as she stood up, stripped off her clothing and went into the bathroom to take a long, hot shower. When she came out of the bathroom, wearing only a thick, fluffy, white towel wrapped around her torso, because she had not packed her robe, she felt refreshed and a little less sad. *Today is a new day*, she told herself aloud, and she planned to put one foot in front of the other in order to try to move on. Being alone on the beach didn't feel like she was running away, it just felt necessary to get away. To find peace. To mend.

Still wearing only a towel, with her dark, wavy, wet hair hanging loose and past her shoulders, Kerrigan walked down the short hallway, through the living room and into the kitchen to retrieve a Diet Coke from the refrigerator. *This summer would be the perfect opportunity for me to start eating healthy,* Kerrigan thought as she placed the cold Diet Coke can on the kitchen table to open it. Her thumb ended up inside of the open can as she looked up to find the door of her beach house opening. She had not heard a knock or a key in the door and she was certain she locked it last night, and that is when she saw Hallie barging in through the door in her muu-muu dress, this one royal blue, and those Birkenstock sandals.

"What the hell?" Kerrigan exclaimed, feeling self-conscious and quickly tightening her towel around herself. "This is my house, I'm naked for chrissakes! Have you lost your mind?" Kerrigan was annoyed and angry and awfully embarrassed as she noticed Hallie coming toward her with a plate of food. It was obviously hot, because she was wearing one red and white striped oven mitt on her left hand as she carried scrambled eggs, two biscuits with gravy smothered on top, and three slices of bacon on a plate into the kitchen and placed it on the table.

"I sure didn't mean to frighten you, honey. I used the master key. I just needed to get this plate of food to you while it's hot. Oh, and think nothing of being nearly naked in front me. God knows I've seen it all. You know how it is, if you've seen one ass, you've seen 'em all."

It took everything Kerrigan had to keep from rolling her eyes at this woman. "I didn't ask for you to cook for me. I'm really not much of a breakfast person anyway," Kerrigan said as she looked down at the plate of food which not only looked good to her, but smelled absolutely delicious. She had not eaten anything substantial in days.

"Just eat before it gets cold," Hallie said as she started to back out of the kitchen, coughing and smiling at the same time. "There's no need for me to stay while you eat, honey. Just enjoy, and bring me my damn plate back later, will ya? That's part of my good china that Stanley and I got for a wedding gift." Kerrigan looked down at what was probably a sixty-year-old plate, nodded her head and waited until Hallie was completely out of her house with the door closed before she sat down at the kitchen table in only her towel, breathing a sigh of relief that she was gone. Then, she ate the entire plate of food. She kept thinking to herself *what a pain in the ass this landlady is*. And Kerrigan's last thought, as she chewed and swallowed her final bite, was *but she sure can cook*.

***

After Kerrigan ate her unexpected breakfast, she felt better. She had not eaten much at all in the past few weeks. She's had no appetite. Nothing tasted good, or sounded worth the trouble to make. She felt unbearably sad and only picked at the food their friends and family brought over and never finished any of the carry-out meals that Keith had talked her into a couple of times. Today, however, Hallie's rude entrance for a kind and generous reason had not gone unnoticed to Kerrigan. Maybe the old woman, with arms too flabby for the cap sleeves on her muu-muu, had a hunch for what Kerrigan needed right now. That still didn't change the fact that Hallie latched onto Kerrigan's nerves like no one else ever has.

***

An hour later, Kerrigan had blow-dried her hair and pulled it up into a messy knot on top of her head. She got dressed in another pair of athletic shorts, this pair was gray, and a pale pink t-shirt. She found her tennis shoes, and put on her sunglasses as she walked out of the door onto the deck. Taking another walk was the only thing on her agenda today.

She found the beach calming, the sound of the waves rushing had a positive effect on her, and she wanted to keep pumping her mind and her heart with that good feeling. She wondered why she felt so drawn to the beach, she really had no connection as she had grown up in Baltimore and never taken too many vacations. She did travel to Destin, Florida with her foster family when she was in junior high school and she remembered that trip well. It was with Gail Boyd's family.

The Boyds became Kerrigan's fourth and last foster family when she was eight years old. She spent ten years with them before leaving for college and never moving back into their home. They never officially adopted her and no other families had come along to pull her away from the Boyds. Kerrigan liked Jerry and Dottie Boyd, but she never bonded with them enough to truly love them like parents. She often wondered why they kept her around, as a part of their family, and then one day about a year after Kerrigan had been living with them, Gail explained why.

Kerrigan reminded the Boyds of their first-born daughter whom they lost at ten years old when she was hit and killed by a car while riding her bicycle. Marti was a chubby girl who always took a backseat to her peers. She was fun to be around, but she was never the life of the party. And that, too, was Kerrigan. The Boyds took good care of her, treating her as well as their own daughter, and Kerrigan responded to that. She just wanted to feel like she belonged somewhere. Gail loved having her around. They were friends who felt more like sisters and Kerrigan often covered for Gail when she was up to no good – making cheat-sheets for tests, staying out past her curfew, smoking cigarettes, experimenting with drugs, and losing her virginity to Keith Ross.

Some things had not changed for Gail. She still, as an adult, managed to be a scene-stealer in every situation. She studied performing arts in college and thrived. After college, however, she never pursued a career in drama, she just lived it. Gail moved back to Baltimore at the age of twenty-three when her parents died in a car collision with a train. Gail inherited their house, their cars, and their entire estate. Nothing was left to Kerrigan in their will because she was not their biological child. At that time, fifteen years after the Boyds had welcomed Kerrigan into their home and into their family, she again questioned why they ever chose to raise her. Maybe it was to fill a void. Maybe they just wanted companionship for Gail. Kerrigan never held a grudge toward Gail after she moved into her parents' house and lived well on what they left behind, only for her. Gail dabbled in careers, but never truly worked a day in her life. She had the money, and made the time, to take very good care of herself. Eventually, she fell into co-ownership of a popular gym, located in downtown Baltimore.

Kerrigan loved and always supported Gail throughout their twenty-year friendship. She was not the type of person to be jealous or hateful. Kerrigan and Keith worked hard for everything they owned, while Gail still had the silver spoon from birth, stuck in her mouth.

So why is Keith Ross good enough for Gail now when he never was before? Kerrigan thought to herself as she strolled the beach. She picked up her pace every now and then, hoping for physical fitness to creep its way into her body this summer. Kerrigan didn't want to dwell on the two of them. She was the one who walked away, knowing they would turn to each other. They already had. Maybe Keith was the one who Gail always wanted. She's had affairs with married men and even dated much younger men she picked up at the gym, but nothing ever lasted with Gail. She enjoyed the hunt for a man, but once she had those men, she broke their hearts. She dropped them in record time and the fault was never hers.

Kerrigan was the only constant in Gail's life. She always stayed in her corner, even when their other friends warned and questioned her about giving Gail complete loyalty. They could clearly see Gail as heartless and chose to keep her at arm's length. Kerrigan had finally learned the hard way how her best friend always gets what she wants, regardless of who she hurts. And now Kerrigan was the one hurting.

The beach was a little more crowded today as Kerrigan made her way to the five-mile marker and turned around to head back. A ten-mile walk was a huge accomplishment for her, considering she had steered clear of any form of exercise her entire life. Not that it mattered to her what day it was, but Kerrigan realized it was Saturday, as she walked back and saw more families together with children of all ages enjoying the sun, sand, and the ocean water. There were more condos and hotels than houses further down the beach from where Kerrigan was staying so she assumed the people she came across were vacationers.

Kerrigan wondered where she would go once her *vacation* was over at summer's end. She no longer had a home, or anyone to be with. *One day at a time*, she reminded herself as she saw a man running ahead on the beach and coming toward her.

She wasn't staring behind her sunglasses, but she was aware of her surroundings. The man had a large, solid build with broad shoulders and a close-shaved head. She could see short blonde hairs – like peach fuzz – all over his head and face. With the exception of his close-cropped beard, he had the appearance of a military man. He looked like if he stopped working out, he could easily get fat. Kerrigan felt *fat* as he passed her with a nod and she managed to utter, "Good morning," almost under her breath.

Seeing other human beings push themselves and their bodies to the point of exertion sometimes has a domino effect. It never had before for Kerrigan, but this time she found herself walking a little faster and eventually she sprinted for a few minutes down the beach. She could have used a sports bra as her own heavy chest came close to knocking her out a few times, and she needed to be aware of her breathing and find a pace that worked for her. *Everyone has to start somewhere*, she thought to herself as she came to a stop, holding her left side. *People actually enjoy this?* Running, even as a kid, always ended up giving her a side ache.

As Kerrigan reached the beach house, she was still out of breath and squeezing her side. Then, she spotted

Hallie, sitting on *her* deck. Kerrigan wondered why Hallie didn't mind her own business, on her own deck, as she stepped up and tried to breathlessly say, "Hello, Hallie."

"Rome wasn't built in one day, you know!" Hallie said to Kerrigan and Kerrigan glared at her.

"And what does that mean?" Kerrigan asked.

"It means I saw you trying to kill yourself out there running on the beach." Kerrigan sat down in the chair beside Hallie, not because she wanted to be close to this woman, but because she felt as if her own legs were going to fall off.

"I guess you could say exercise and I are new to each other," Kerrigan said, attempting to smile.

"I prefer to remain strangers with it," Hallie responded, laughing at herself, and Kerrigan smiled.

"Well, I've decided to incorporate a walk, or maybe even a jog, into my days out here this summer," Kerrigan said, feeling more at ease with this older woman because her intentions seemed sincere and her wit was entertaining.

"You do what you need to do to get your mind off of what brought you here by yourself, honey." And that was all Hallie said to her as she got up out of her chair and walked off the deck. She coughed all the way back to her house, and Kerrigan could still hear her through an open window in her kitchen as she now stood up from the chair on the deck. She wanted to go inside and drink some water, as opposed to a Diet Coke this time, but before she opened the door to her beach house she again saw that bulky man running back down the beach. He was dripping in sweat, but clearly was not struggling to run like she had been. His light gray running shorts were sweat-soaked in the front appearing as if he peed himself and his red, dry-fit sleeveless shirt looked as if it could have been rung out. He kept his eyes on the path in front of him as Kerrigan stared, without her sunglasses on this time. She was mesmerized by his ability to run. The man looked like a machine, and Kerrigan wondered if he was some sort of trainer. If she had any money, she would hire him – or someone like him – to teach her endurance like that.

What Kerrigan did not expect to see next was that same man slowing down, and eventually turning to finish his run at the first beach house on the other side of Hallie's. He lived there. He's her neighbor.

***

Kerrigan went back inside of her house, chugged sixteen ounces of iced water in a glass and noticed Hallie's plate on the kitchen counter. It was clean and ready to be returned. This time, Kerrigan decided she would interrupt Hallie at her house. She grinned to herself as she left her beach house and walked through the sand and over to Hallie's. *Should I knock or just barge in?* Kerrigan almost laughed out loud when she raised her closed fist and knocked twice on the door.

It took a couple minutes before Hallie made her way to the door and opened it. "Your plate, ma'am." Kerrigan said, handing it over to her.

"Oh, I guess this is your way of tellin' me you need a refill?" Hallie asked her, still standing in the doorway as Kerrigan remained outside.

"No. I just want to thank you for breakfast this morning. It was the best meal I've had in a long time." What Kerrigan really meant to say was, it was the only meal she had *tasted* in a long time. It was something so trivial, it was a plate of food, but a part of her felt as if she was coming back to life again. It may have not even been the food, but Kerrigan was not ready to admit it could be the company on the beach. A part of her really didn't mind her neighbor, Hallie.

"Why don't you come inside, stay awhile. There is so much you and I do not know about each other," Hallie suggested, and Kerrigan hesitated. The older woman sensed Kerrigan's uncertainty so she spoke again. "Or better yet, let it be my turn to tell you about my life." When Hallie stepped back from the doorway, still sporting her Birkenstocks indoors, Kerrigan accepted her invitation to come inside.

And when she did, she saw the living room decorated, almost to the point of being cluttered, with framed pictures. There were pictures on every inch of the coffee table in front of the sofa and also on an end table in between the sofa and the recliner. All of the frames were silver and some of the pictures in them were black and white, which Kerrigan thought truly complimented the photos.

"Who are they?" Kerrigan asked, walking closer to get a better look. "Your children?" So many of the pictures included three beautiful girls, probably in their early twenties. Two were tall, thin blondes and a third was stocky with a round face and dark hair and she looked like she could have been a young Hallie.

"My daughters, my beautiful girls," Hallie answered with a sadness in her voice.

"They don't live around here?" Kerrigan asked as she set one frame down and picked up another. It was almost like being in a personal museum, the life of Hallie. There also was an old wedding picture where a young Hallie stood with locked arms next to a tall, thin man with a head of thick blond hair and Kerrigan instantly saw the resemblance from the photographs of two of their daughters.

"They are pretty damn far away and have been for the last twenty-three years," Hallie replied. Kerrigan looked confused and she stopped glancing at the photos all around the room just as she noticed there were more set up on a table against the wall. "Tara was a therapist, Tori was a teacher, and Tess was a photographer. She took most of the pictures I have." Kerrigan didn't understand as Hallie spoke of her daughters in the past tense, but she continued to listen.

"Twenty-three years ago, it was my sixtieth birthday." Kerrigan quickly did the math and figured Hallie to now be eighty-three years old. She has seen the deep wrinkles on her face, but right now she looked older than Kerrigan had ever noticed before. "My girls all lived in Chicago at the time and they insisted on coming home to celebrate. A boyfriend of my oldest, Tara, was going to fly them home in his tiny private plane. He had just enough seats for the four of them. I didn't like the idea, but I was so excited about seeing my girls and having them all home at the same time, that I just kept my fears to myself." Kerrigan's eyes were wide as Hallie told her the plane crashed en route and not a single passenger survived. All of her girls died that night, and the cause was later detected as a fuel gauge malfunction. "The son of bitch flying my girls ran out of gas in midair," Hallie cursed with tears in her eyes. No matter how many years have passed, the pain obviously remained, and was still terribly raw.

"Oh my God," Kerrigan exclaimed, covering her mouth with her hand. She wanted to reach out to this woman. She wanted to cling to her and tell her how she knows the pain of burying a child, a baby. *But three? How could this woman have ever managed to move on without all of her children?*

"Yes, *my God*. He did this to me and my husband…and then my poor husband's health declined. He was never the same after we lost our girls, and he gave up and went to join them less than two years later." Hallie shook her head. "It's true what they say, men are such wuses. But, I always say I was born with two hearts…because the day I lost my girls, one completely shattered. And then the day Stanley left me behind, the other one broke. It's still ticking, but sometimes I wish it wouldn't be so I could join my family. I think if I had a garage on this beach house, I'd close it up with my car in it and start the engine."

"Hallie!" Kerrigan exclaimed, scolding her but understanding exactly how she feels.

"Oh honey, I'm only teasing… I don't even own a damn car anymore." Hallie laughed out loud and that ignited a coughing spell for which she excused herself to go into the kitchen for a glass of water. Kerrigan stayed behind in the living room, continuing to look at the pictures. The pictures of the loved ones Hallie lost. Each and every one of them.

When Hallie returned to the living room after having soothed her cough, she sat down in her recliner chair and watched Kerrigan walk around the room. "My girls were twenty, twenty-two, and twenty-four."

"Are you mad at God?" Kerrigan asked. "I mean, your comment earlier struck me as you blamed him… and maybe still do." Kerrigan was struggling with that herself. How could an almighty and powerful God allow this to happen to an innocent baby? A baby she tried so hard to conceive, carry full-term, and finally bring into this world.

"I was…for a very long time," Hallie replied. "I consider myself a woman of great faith, and the God I believe in allowed something to happen to me that tore me apart to my very core. I never thought I'd survive that kind of loss, let alone ever want to pray to the heavens again."

"But, you did?" Kerrigan was begging for some type of hope from this woman, pleading from deep inside of her soul for some help getting out of the quicksand she was sinking deeper into.

"I did, and I did it for myself. I didn't want to continue feeling so heartless. It's an isolating, destructive feeling and I refused to stay in that dark place. It took me years, my husband was already gone too by the time I said to myself, 'Hallie, it's high time to live again.' I now allow my wonderful memories of my girls and my Stanley to carry me through the pain. Believe me, I still have my days and sometimes I still let God have it for taking all of them away from me. I no longer raise my fists to the heavens at him anymore. Instead, when I feel beaten and lost and angry, I get down on my knees beside my bed – because that is the only place I can be sure to get myself back up again – and I scold him a little and then I beg him to point me in the direction of my purpose. There has to be a reason why I'm still here."

There were tears in Kerrigan's eyes as she listened to this amazing old woman share her heartbreaking story of loss. She turned her head so Hallie would not see the tears free-falling down her cheeks. At eighty-three years old, this woman had a purpose alright. But, Kerrigan didn't know if she was ready to allow Hallie to find it, to allow her to teach her how to heal. Not just yet.

Chapter 4

Kerrigan stayed with Hallie for hours. It was early evening when she returned to her beach house. It had been *one of those days* for Hallie, she had said to Kerrigan as the two of them shared turkey club sandwiches that Kerrigan helped Hallie prepare for lunch. This time, Kerrigan wanted to stay and eat with Hallie and she wanted to be the listening ear she obviously needed today.

Hallie never asked her why, but there were times throughout the day when Kerrigan cried as Hallie talked about her daughters and how isolated she has felt without them all these years. Kerrigan wondered if she will ever be able to open up about losing Piper. Right now, it was still too painful for her to talk about.

As she walked into her bedroom, Kerrigan saw the yellow baby blanket lying on her unmade bed. And then she remembered going back for it after she had been on the road for an hour following her rush to pack in her bedroom once she witnessed Keith and Gail get too close on her living room couch.

She recalled the moment when she heard the front door of her house close and she walked out of her bedroom, carrying her suitcase. She watched Keith turn around from closing the door after Gail had left and his eyes immediately were fixed on the suitcase in Kerrigan's hand.

"What are you doing, Kerri?" A part of him wanted to run to her, beg her to stay. But, he didn't. He just stood there, looking at her from across their living room in the house they called *theirs* for five years, and he knew his wife could not be talked out of this. She was already gone. Their marriage was already over. And it had been since the day their baby girl died.

"I think you know," Kerrigan replied. "It never was me, was it?"

"What?" Keith looked perplexed, but felt guilty.

"The way you look at her, the way she must feel in your arms again after all these years. I know you Keith Ross, I know you've always wanted her." Kerrigan remained calm, but this new pain that surfaced was devastating.

Keith didn't try to talk his way out of what his wife obviously saw. He just said, "I'm sorry."

"Me too," Kerrigan said to her husband. "I'm sorry I ever fell for you. I'm sorry I believed you wanted me. I guess it's clear now. I was the one with the greater need. I wanted you around more than you wanted to be. I wanted a baby so badly, and you just appeased me."

"That's not true," Keith interrupted her and moved quickly across the room to face her, and stand close. "I wanted to be a daddy, I wanted her..." he choked on his words as his bottom lip began to tremble. "I loved Piper and we would have given her the best life, together as a family." Kerrigan had been able to hold her composure until the conversation turned to their baby. She had tears welling up in her eyes and a knot which hurt in her throat.

"I know you loved her," Kerrigan said, through her tears that began free-falling. "And I also know you love Gail. Make a life with her, for as long as *she* will have you." And those were the last words Kerrigan said to her husband before she walked out of their home, and away from their marriage. She heard his every word as he followed her outside to her jeep. *"Don't do this without telling me where you are going! At least call me when you get there, so I know you're safe."* They did not have a garage, just a narrow rock driveway where both of their cars were parked, one behind the other. Keith's small pick-up truck was blocking her jeep, but she started up her vehicle anyway as he stood there barefoot in jeans, uncomfortably lifting up his feet, one and then the other, on the rocks. She turned the steering wheel of her jeep in the opposite direction from where she left her husband standing, and she purposely drove right through the lawn in their front yard to get out of there. She never looked back. She didn't want to see him standing there, in the dark with only the outside porch light shining.

She had only been on the road for an hour when she turned around. She had packed in a hurry and thought she had everything she needed. But, there was one thing she wanted. One thing she could not leave behind.

As Kerrigan pulled back onto the rock in their driveway, she shifted her jeep into park right behind Gail's sport utility vehicle. It had only been two hours since she left. It had not taken her husband long to call *her* back, and Kerrigan was sure Gail didn't waste any time running to him.

All she wanted to do was go inside and get that blanket. That meant having to open the closed door to her baby's nursery, which was something she had not been able to do since the dreadful day her baby was carried out of that room, lifeless.

When Kerrigan opened the front door to the home she shared with Keith, the first person she saw standing in the doorway of the kitchen was Gail. And she looked startled to see Kerrigan back so soon.

"I'm here because Keith-" Gail started to explain and Kerrigan cut her off. "Keith needed you. I get that." Kerrigan's words were cold, but Gail seemed unaffected.

"He needs someone to be here for him right now, and you can't seem to bring yourself to be that person anymore." Gail's words were heartless. She may as well have just said she wants to be that person for Keith, because she is the better woman for him.

"I just lost my baby," Kerrigan said, remaining calm and never taking her eyes off of her best friend since childhood.

"No, Piper was not only *your* baby. She was Keith's, too," Gail almost spat those words at Kerrigan. "This is not all about you again, Kerrigan. I know how you love with everything you've got. I've seen you throw yourself to the wind. It's overwhelming sometimes, and maybe your husband has finally had enough of this being all about you."

"Are you serious? Do you even hear yourself? You are a heartless bitch! I was her mother. I have a right to grieve my heart out. All you care about is my husband and you are turning this tragedy into something sick. He is vulnerable and you are taking advantage of him!" Kerrigan raised her voice at Gail and she saw Keith walking out of the bedroom.

"That is enough!" He screamed at both of them, and then Kerrigan walked past him and down the hallway. She ended up standing directly in front of the closed nursery door. She put one hand on the door knob, but had not turned and opened the door. She felt Keith and Gail watching her from behind. She had to do this. *Just go in there and get it, and then walk out of here with what little strength you have left.* And so she did.

The room still smelled the same. Like a baby. Her baby. She found the yellow blanket folded once and draped over the crib's railing. It felt soft in her hands as she took it, held it close, suppressed the urge to cry, and walked out of the room. There was nothing else she wanted. All of the clothes in the closet would only remind her of how her baby never had the chance to grow, to live.

When she walked into the living room, she intended to bolt out of the door, but she couldn't. She found herself taking deliberate, almost slow-motion-like, steps. Keith was sitting on the couch, bent forward, with his face in his hands, and Gail was standing in front of him. She wouldn't dare touch him in front of her, again, Kerrigan thought. But, then she said to herself, *why not, he's always been hers anyway.* He carried her in his heart since the day she first sunk her claws into him and he never stopped pining away for her. *She is something else. What a woman.* Kerrigan loved her and looked past her true character for far too long.

"If you want him, for once in your life make a choice and stick with it," Kerrigan said, making full, affectionless eye contact with Gail. "Stop hurting people. Make me the last person on your long list of people you've thrown away." Gail's eyes were wide and she never uttered a word as Kerrigan walked out of her own home. Keith, *the coward,* had not moved from the couch. He never fought for her, or for their marriage, and that alone spoke volumes to Kerrigan.

***

Kerrigan was sitting on the side of the sleigh bed, holding the blanket on her lap. *"There is just too much loss in the world, and you know I've carried more than my share,"* she said aloud to herself, and to God. *"Help me get past the pain, God. Please."* That was the first prayer she had said since her baby died. She swore she would never again talk to God after her begging and pleading fell on deaf ears. All she wanted, all she asked for, was for God to save her baby the morning she found Piper already gone. But, he had not helped her. And now, Kerrigan startled herself when she asked God for help again.

Chapter 5

The next morning, Kerrigan was on the beach again. She walked, she jogged, she panted and she hurt, but she kept moving. This was now where she felt most comfortable. Under the sun and in the sand near the water was where she could completely let herself go and not feel as lost in her grief. She was hardly a person anyone would call fit, but Kerrigan relished this new feeling of pushing her body to move and to bend. Her muscles were sore in places she never even knew she had muscle, and Kerrigan felt the burn as she sat down on the bottom step at the end of her deck, with her feet still in the sand. She was wearing tennis shoes, and she took them off to empty out the sand.

She left her shoes and no-show socks behind on the deck as she walked through the sand, out into the ocean. The water felt chilly on her feet and ankles while she stood there looking as far out into the ocean as her eyes allowed. She never realized she wasn't alone out there until she looked to the side and saw a man, drenched in sweat, slipping barefoot out of his running shoes and leaving them in the sand as he made his way into the water. She watched him swim, *damn his arms are long and his hands and feet are huge.* Again, Kerrigan admired this man's athletic abilities. She never took her eyes off of him the whole time he swam, and she was still staring when he came out of the water and saw her.

"Hi," Kerrigan said, waving her left hand in the air as he walked through the sand.

"Morning," he responded, and that was all he said. *Rude or shy?* Kerrigan wondered, as she started walking back to her own beach house. And that's when he stopped her. "So where's MJ? I see you're staying at her place." Kerrigan turned around to find that man holding his tennis shoes, and dripping wet with ocean water this time.

"She's backpacking across Europe." It was no joke. MJ did things like that, and most of the time it was spur of the moment actions. In this case, her being gone from her home for the summer, benefited Kerrigan. When MJ called her up after the funeral to offer her deepest sympathy for losing Piper, she, like everyone else, offered to help in any way. MJ then informed her that her beach house would be empty if she needed a getaway during the summer. At the moment,

Kerrigan had not paid much attention to her offer. After she walked out on her marriage, however, she called MJ from the road and told her she needed to stay at the beach house for the entire summer.

"Seriously?" the runner asked Kerrigan as he laughed out loud. "Not that it surprises me about MJ, but wow. We should all be so lucky to live like there's no tomorrow." As he started to walk away, Kerrigan realized this man was neither shy nor rude. He was a stranger who lived just a house away from her, and she wondered how well MJ knew him. She spoke again to get his attention before he continued walking away.

"So you live here, in the first beach house?" Kerrigan pointed past Hallie's house.

"Yes, I do," he answered, offering no other information.

"It's nice here, very peaceful," Kerrigan added.

"So you're not from around here?" he asked her.

"No, I'm not. I live in Baltimore. I've lived there since I was eight years old. I only remember living in one other city, St. Louis, when I was five or six years old." Whether or not she would return to living in Baltimore was in question. There was nothing left for her there. She needed to get a job, eventually, but she could find one anywhere. She didn't want to think about returning to being a paramedic. Time would tell her direction, and in the meantime she was living rent-free on the beach and spending very little of the money which had to last her for the summer.

"I've been there, to St. Louis," he clarified. "It's the home of the St. Louis Cardinals, the team that always seems to end up in the World Series."

"You know it!" Kerrigan heard herself exclaim those words. She loved sports, and being able to express that always enabled her to feel comfortable around men. That was how it all began with Keith. She was not thinking of Keith now though. She was thinking how nice it was to have some human contact. She had thought seclusion on the beach was what she needed, day and night, but getting to know Hallie and now talking to her other neighbor, was simply nice.

"Do you have a name or should I just call you Fredbird?" Kerrigan laughed out loud at his comment. "Fred for short, please," she responded and he laughed at her. "Okay then, Fred it is. It's nice to meet you, Fred. I'm Nate."

"Nate, huh?" Kerrigan asked, smiling at him.

"What? Do you have a problem with my name?" he asked, curiously.

"No, not at all. Nate is a very nice name. "

"But…?"

"I just expected a big, bulked up man like you to have a masculine name."

"A masculine name? Such as?"

"Oh I don't know, like Jake or John," Kerrigan offered, still smiling and feeling surprisingly comfortable joking with this man. She had not felt this lighthearted in weeks. "Nate just makes me think of a computer geek."

"I do work with computers," Nate informed her. "I have one in my squad car."

"You're a police officer?" Kerrigan asked him. She had not seen a police car parked anywhere near the beach, but she had driven only once since she arrived and that was to make a trip to the grocery store.

"Yes, I am."

"Well, I'll try not to break any laws while I'm here this summer," Kerrigan teased him.

"Yes, please, be mindful and be a good girl at all times," Nate teased her, and she thought *a good girl, of course, that's me*. Kerrigan wanted to continue their conversation, maybe ask him if he lives in the beach house alone, but then she wondered if that would make her seem too nosy. He was not wearing a wedding ring, but leaving jewelry behind during a run was not so unusual. Kerrigan had left her wedding ring behind on the dresser top in the bedroom she shared with Keith.

"I will let you enjoy this beautiful day," Nate said, as he began to walk away from Kerrigan. "Thank you, you too," she replied as he walked toward his home and she stepped up on the deck to go inside of her temporary home.

After taking a Diet Coke out of the refrigerator, she

stepped outside again to sit on the deck and sip the addiction she's had for most of her adult life. And before long, before she gave in to the urge to close her eyes behind her dark sunglasses, she saw Hallie making her way over.

"Hi honey, mind if I join you?" Hallie asked, already coming up onto the deck and plopping down in a chair. Today, her muu-muu was yellow. Kerrigan wondered if she had one in every color of the rainbow and beyond. "Sure, go ahead," Kerrigan replied.

"Listen, I just wanna apologize for my dumpy-ass mood yesterday. I shouldn't have brought you into all of that." Hallie seemed sincere, and Kerrigan finally opened up to her. "Your story, your pain helped me to see how life is unbearable for all of us sometimes, not just some of us. I no longer feel so alone in my grief now, Hallie, and that is because of you."

Hallie looked at her long and hard. She never wore sunglasses so she was squinting in Kerrigan's direction. "Whenever you're ready, honey, I will listen."

"I know you will, Hallie, but I need more time. Just talk to me about anything or anyone else right now," Kerrigan said, still feeling uncomfortable and afraid to share her grief.

"Anyone else? How about that hottie who lives next door to me? I've been telling Nate for awhile now that he can come over and cuff me anytime!" Hallie said, laughing and coughing. To her, Nate was not necessarily in the category of *a hottie*, and Kerrigan giggled at the thought of

Hallie thinking so. He had a big, strong body, a close-shaved head and a scruffy, but kind face. His suntan looked attractive and Kerrigan was trying to work on getting one of her own. Her time on the deck was helping to give her some color, but she needed to hold her breath to get into her swimsuit and head down to the sand for some real sun. Getting the courage to do that seemed unthinkable to Kerrigan right now. She didn't like seeing herself naked, so why would she pain anyone else by making them see her half naked in a swimsuit?

"Nate is a good man, also not without his share of heartache," Hallie said, as Kerrigan wondered what he has been through, but refrained from asking. "You know, I think it's just bullshit how we are all expected to deal with so much pain in our lives. They say it's supposed to make us stronger though…" Hallie's words trailed off as she and Kerrigan were sitting there, sharing silence and thinking the same thing. *Tragedies can bring people to their knees.* They've both been there, and there are days when feeling strong, or even feeling capable of going on anymore, just doesn't happen.

***

Kerrigan spent the rest of the day and evening alone. It was dinner time and she hadn't felt like eating, so she took another Diet Coke out of the refrigerator, noticing there were only three left, and made a mental note to go to the store tomorrow. She ended up outside again, sitting in one of the chairs on the deck with her soda can placed on the small table in between the two chairs. This wasn't getting any easier. She knew there was no truth to being able to run from problems, heartache, and especially grief. It did feel comforting to be so far away from her failed marriage and the destruction of her two decades of friendship with Gail Boyd. She wanted to move on from both of them. She believed she would eventually get over them, but would she ever move past the pain of losing her baby girl? *Never*.

Kerrigan heard voices from where she sat on the deck and when she looked up, she saw Nate walking in the sand with a little girl, wearing a pink sundress and small pink flip flops to match. He spotted Kerrigan too and then he and the child walked up onto the deck.

"Hi Fred, how are you tonight?" Nate said, teasing Kerrigan as she stood up to meet his guest, wondering if she was his.

"Her name is Fred?" the little girl asked Nate aloud, while looking up at Kerrigan with a funny look on her face. She had red curly hair, and a bridge of freckles across her nose and cheeks. *How adorable*, Kerrigan thought.

"No, sweet girl, my name is Kerrigan. What's your name?"

"I'm Meggie and I'm four years old." Meggie held out her hand for Kerrigan to shake it. Kerrigan smiled, impressed with her manners, and took her little hand in hers. That is when Kerrigan felt how sticky her hand was and she laughed to herself, noticing the box of lemonheads in Meggie's other hand, and more than one stuffed into the side of her mouth.

"It's nice to meet you, Meggie. Do you like lemonheads?" Kerrigan asked as she looked up at Nate, rolling his eyes while Meggie nodded her head. "She is addicted to candy, especially those lemonheads and her mom always lets her have them," Nate explained, and Kerrigan wondered if *her mom* was still in the picture, in Nate's life. But, again, she didn't want to pry.

"Oh that's alright, we all have some sort of addiction. See that soda can over there on the table?" Kerrigan pointed and asked Meggie as she again nodded her head. "That is my addiction. I absolutely cannot live without my Diet Coke." As Kerrigan said those words, both Nate and Meggie giggled. And then she thought about how silly that sounded. She absolutely could not live without Diet Coke? It was more like she absolutely could not live without her baby girl. But, she now had to. Kerrigan tried not to appear somber in front of the child as Nate spoke next. "Meggie is my daughter. She stays with me every weekend."

"That is wonderful, how lucky you are to have such a beautiful little girl, Nate. And how lucky you are, sweet girl, to have such a big, strong daddy to take care of you." Kerrigan said, thinking Nate must be divorced from Meggie's mother.

"I'm the lucky one," Nate said, watching Meggie stuff two more lemonheads into her mouth and then telling her to eat "one at a time."

"We are going for a walk on the beach," Meggie exclaimed, "but my daddy wanted to say hi to you first."

"Hi," Kerrigan said, looking up at Nate who had to be at least six-foot-two because she was five-foot-eight and had never felt short, but next to this man she did. Nate laughed at Kerrigan again, and she instantly had that familiar carefree feeling with him. It began when he started calling her Fred and she liked joking around with him. He took her mind off of her pain.

"Daddy! Let's walk." Meggie made her way down the deck and stepped off into the sand as Nate watched her. "I will be right there. Play in the sand for a minute." Kerrigan wondered why he had not followed her as he turned to ask her a question that surprised her, "Would you like to have a drink sometime?"

"What? Me?" Kerrigan instantly felt uncomfortable. She is a married woman, well not for much longer, but she did not feel comfortable being asked out on a date. She didn't date much in high school and then in college, she and Keith eased into their relationship and neither one of them had asked the other out on a date. They just fell into bed one night, where Kerrigan lost her virginity to Keith, four years after Gail had. "I don't know what to say," Kerrigan felt flustered.

"It's just a drink, we can have Diet Coke if you want?" Nate smiled.

"Maybe sometime," she finally was able to answer him.

"I'll take that, thank you," Nate said. "I didn't mean to assume you are single. I should have used my manners and asked you first."

"It's fine," Kerrigan answered vaguely. With that, she noticed Hallie walking on her beach house deck, focused on something down in the sand, and then she began to run. She looked out of breath, and most likely she was, as she was waving her arms and yelling to catch the attention of both Kerrigan and Nate. At the same time, both of them made out the words she was screaming, "Meggie! It's Meggie! Something is wrong!" Nate spun his head around and Kerrigan immediately glanced in the direction of where the little girl had been playing in the sand. She was down on her knees, grabbing her throat with her hands and Nate took off running the length of the deck to get to her. Kerrigan followed, but her steps felt motionless. When she reached the end of the deck, she saw Meggie turning blue and Nate panicked. "She's choking!" he screamed and then he froze.

"Call an ambulance!" Hallie directed that order to Kerrigan and Kerrigan didn't move either. Her cell phone was tucked away in a drawer inside of the beach house, still powered off and the battery was most likely in need of a charge. She knew better than to run from an emergency, like this, where every second counts. She was trained for emergencies. She needed to act, she needed to help. She had to put her failed attempt to save Piper out of her mind. It was the last time she had administered CPR and she swore she would never do it again on anyone. *Every second matters. Do it. Help her!*

Kerrigan jumped off the end of the deck, missing the two steps and one foot landed on the empty box of lemonheads. And that is when she sprung into action. She pulled Meggie away from Nate, who had just picked her up from the sand. The candy was either lodged in her throat or windpipe, and it was definitely blocking her air flow. Kerrigan acted quickly to prevent the choking from cutting off the oxygen to her brain and her losing consciousness. First, with the heel of her hand, she gave Meggie five back blows between her little shoulder blades. Then, she gave her five abdominal thrusts, also known as the Heimlich maneuver. Those thrusts were quick and upward and Kerrigan alternated this twice before, finally, all three of the adults saw two lemonheads, which were fused together, fly out of the little girl's mouth and land in the sand.

Meggie immediately began crying hysterically as Nate took her into his arms and held her, so tight and close. He had tears on his face, a face which wore shock. His sheer shock in this situation forced him to block out his own CPR training as a police officer. He suddenly felt embarrassed, but incredibly grateful to Kerrigan for her quick response.

"Oh dear Lord, her crying is music to my ears. You saved her, Kerrigan!" Hallie was near tears as Nate looked at Kerrigan. "Thank you! You saved my baby girl's life." Those words seared through Kerrigan as she backed up, closer to the deck. She did not respond. She just kept thinking, *your baby girl, your baby girl...Why not my baby girl?*

She walked away, reaching the deck. She couldn't stay there. She heard Hallie's voice, calling her. She heard Nate ask if he should get Meggie checked out at the hospital. All of their attempts to reach Kerrigan fell on deaf ears. She heard Meggie's crying, over and over, as she walked into the beach house and closed the door behind her. What she wouldn't have given *that day* to have heard Piper Rose's cries after her repeated attempts to save her life.

***

Two hours went by and Kerrigan was sitting in the dark on the couch in her living room. The tears never came. She just sat there, with that same sickening feeling in the pit of her stomach. She had not been able to save her baby. Her baby was gone. How unfair. How incredibly crippling of a feeling it was for her to save another man's baby girl, but she could not save her own. She now hated the career she once felt she was born to do.

Kerrigan was brought out of her thoughts, her sorrow, at the sound of a soft knock at the door. She didn't get up to answer it, and after one more knock, this one louder, the door opened. She looked up to see a large figure standing in her doorway. It was dark and she would have been scared, but she knew it was him.

"Can I come in?"

"You shouldn't be here. You need to be with your daughter. She is a gift, and God just gave her back to you. Don't ever take that for granted." Kerrigan's words almost scared him. He closed the door behind him and walked over to turn on the lamp which sat on a narrow, rectangular-shaped, wooden table against the wall. He then walked closer to Kerrigan, still seated on the couch. Her legs were curled up underneath her and she was holding one of the square, multi-colored, striped decorative pillows on her lap.

"I took Meggie to the emergency room, she checked out fine. I owe you so much for that. I know CPR, my God, I'm a police officer, but I couldn't do it. I panicked and I blanked out, and I don't even want to think about what would have happened if you had not been there."

"No, don't think about it. Take it from me, if you believe the *thought* of it will kill you, try the reality of it." Kerrigan sounded cold and heartless, and Nate wanted to understand what she was saying to him, but he didn't.

"What happened to you, Kerrigan?" It was the first time he had said her name. The jokes were over. She was not Fred. The mood was painfully serious, but he stayed. He didn't want to walk away, but she wished he would have.

"Just go," she said.

"No, I'm not leaving. Meggie is with her mom. When I called her to meet us at the hospital, she refused to let me take Meggie home with me. I gave in, because I don't want this to be a fight for me to get to see her again. We all just need to calm down."

"I prefer to be left alone, Nate," Kerrigan said, feeling out of energy to talk to him, or anyone.

"I can't walk away from you right now. Talk to me. You are dealing with something, I could it see in your actions out there on the beach and now I can see it in your eyes. What in the hell happened to you? What brought you here, a thousand miles from your home, all alone?"

Kerrigan got up off of the couch and walked over to the door. She opened it for him and then spoke, "Please leave me alone."

And that is when Nate gave up. He had to. He was a gentleman, an officer of the law, so he finally did as the lady asked of him. Before leaving, he turned his body to her, looked her in the eyes, and said, "I just wanted to repay you in some way, any way, for what you did for me tonight. You know where to find me, if you ever want to talk."

As Nate walked out of the door, Kerrigan closed it behind him. She closed it fast and hard. She had to, because the tears broke loose immediately and came with heart-wrenching sounds of wailing from someone who was so sick and tired of grieving, of feeling such unbearable loss. She dropped to her knees in front of the closed door and sobbed. And what she didn't know was Nate never really left. He stood on the other side of the door and listened. Her cries broke his heart, but what pained him even more was her resistance to letting him in. He wanted to help her.

Chapter 6

Kerrigan woke up the next morning on the couch. Her face was puffy and red from crying throughout the night. She felt like she had taken a dozen steps backwards since she lost Piper. Since she arrived at the beach house, Kerrigan had found herself feeling a little stronger, at times. And then last night happened.

She felt incredible relief to know Meggie is alright. She even felt more at ease now about being the one who saved her life. Maybe it was the sun peering in the windows through the closed window blinds, signifying a new day. Or maybe she just knew it is time again to attempt putting one foot in front of the other. Kerrigan made her way into the bathroom to take a hot shower.

Afterward, Kerrigan forced herself to eat a piece of dry toast, because she never bought any butter, and then she drank a half of a can of Diet Coke. She needed something in her stomach before she slipped on her beach uniform of shorts, a t-shirt, and tennis shoes and headed outside to walk, to run if her body will allow her to, and to clear her mind.

When Kerrigan turned the door knob and pulled her door open, she didn't have a chance to step out onto her deck because Meggie was standing right in front of her. "Oh, sweet girl, you startled me!" Kerrigan brushed her hand through the loose red curls on top of Meggie's head and then she looked past her and saw Hallie standing at the end of the deck, still in the sand.

"She was just going to leave you a little something by your door," Hallie raised her voice. "I will let her explain."

Kerrigan looked down at Meggie as she handed her a small, brown wicker basket with the long handle, and Kerrigan noticed it was full of candy. Cherry Clans. Jolly Ranchers. Gobstoppers. Starburst. Red licorice. "This is for you," Meggie said. "I'm giving you all my candy for helping me when I choked. I wanted to do something nice for you, and I don't think I should eat it anymore." Meggie spoke slow, but very clear for a child of four years old. Kerrigan thought she and her gesture were both incredibly sweet. "Oh my goodness, Meggie. I love my gift, but I do hope you will come visit me and help me eat all of this. I promise what happened with the lemonheads will never happen again, if you're careful and if adults watch you when you're chewing or have hard candy like that in your mouth," Kerrigan told her.

"I only will eat it if you're with me, Kerrigan," the little girl said as she reached her arms up and around Kerrigan's legs. It was the sweetest hug she had ever received, and if she had allowed herself, she could have cried right then and there. Instead, Kerrigan placed the basket on the deck at her feet and lifted up Meggie into her arms. "Anytime you want to eat candy, you come see me, okay?" Meggie nodded her head as Kerrigan carried her to the end of the deck where Hallie was still waiting.

Hallie told her that Meggie came back to Nate's house this morning. Kerrigan wondered where he was now, but then assumed he felt awkward about last night. She had chased him away when he tried to reach out to her. Hallie never spoke to Kerrigan about what happened on the beach with Meggie. They continued to share small talk and included Meggie in their conversation before the two of them went back to Hallie's house to play Chutes and Ladders while Kerrigan began to walk the beach.

The gulf breeze today felt warm as Kerrigan picked up her pace in the sand. The temperature highs since she arrived had only been in the low to mid eighties, and the nights had been cool. It was a beautiful place to be in the southern tropical area of North America, and Kerrigan was happy to be there despite the pain she felt.

She kept thinking about Gail today. It was one of those days when she could have used her best friend. The two of them were different, complete opposites in fact, but they always found a way to reach each other, help each other, and save each other when one of them had fallen into quicksand. The idea of Gail turning on her so abruptly, choosing Keith over their friendship, over everything, hurt. The night that Kerrigan returned to the home she shared with Keith and found Gail there, acting as if she owned the place – and Keith – had burned her. She would never again be able to turn to her. Letting go of Gail, of Keith, and of Piper was just too much to handle. Kerrigan felt that sick feeling deep inside the pit of her stomach again as she began to run. One foot in front of the other, faster and harder, down the beach. She was not pacing herself, she was breathing too rapidly, and her side ached. But, she pushed herself harder. As she ran, she felt the tears on her face. *Damn them for betraying me. I don't need them anymore. I don't want them in my life. Fuck you, Gail. Fuck you, Keith. And dare I damn a God I believed in, prayed to my entire life? Dare I damn him for giving me a baby I tried so desperately to have, only to take her away from me just weeks later. Five weeks. Five weeks of knowing, experiencing, and truly loving every amazing second spent with my baby girl. My baby girl! She was mine! Damn you all to hell for leaving me feeling so fucking alone!*

Her thoughts raced, her words were loud inside of her head as she continued to run. Kerrigan reached mile marker three before she realized she had just run two miles straight, hard and fast. Her legs felt shaky, she could hear her own pulse inside of her head, pounding in her ears, but her breathing had become more regular and her side no longer ached. She ran and she survived. And what a release she felt doing so. Kerrigan walked two additional miles before turning around to walk back to the beach house.

***

When she reached the deck, she could barely lift up her legs to step up onto it. She made her way to the door of her beach house and she was about to go in, when she heard a voice behind her.

"Forget about going to get a Diet Coke. Water is what you need after that workout." It was Nate and he was standing at the end of her deck, holding a bottle of water. He walked toward her, and attempted to hand it to her.

"Thank you," Kerrigan said, "but I do have water inside." Tap water, not bottled, she thought.

"Why do you do that?" Nate asked her, still holding on to the bottled water.

"Do what?"

"Close off from people who are only trying to help you."

"I guess I am pretty self-sufficient, so I don't need or expect anyone's help." Kerrigan tried to explain, but she could tell she had offended him.

"Well, Miss Self-Sufficient, drink the damn water and be grateful you have neighbors on this beach who want to look out for you." As Nate said those words, he turned around and walked off of the deck. He left the bottle of water behind, on the floor of her deck, where he had been standing. Kerrigan just stood there, watching him. His large build, his incredibly broad shoulders. He was wearing faded jeans, dark brown boat shoes bare foot and a solid navy blue polo shirt. She never said another word to him. She, once again, allowed him to walk away.

Kerrigan didn't go inside after Nate left. She just sat down in the chair on the deck and breathed. That man had a way of stirring her, but her heart was too broken and too sore to let anyone in. Hallie had tried too, and she actually had made some progress with Kerrigan the day she shared her own grief.

Giving these people, her beach neighbors, a chance to get to know her, to try to help her heal, was risky. Kerrigan's experience with caring about and loving other people eventually meant pain. She didn't want to feel alone, and sad, and heartless, but she did. The pain and the loss in her life had caused her to turn cold. *Maybe one day, that will change,* she thought as she sat there, soaking up the sun. But, Kerrigan knows all too well how there are no guarantees in this life. People will hurt you. People will leave you. No matter how much you love them, and need them. Her parents gave her up. Her foster parents died, and left her with nothing. Her baby died. Her husband and her best friend, together, betrayed her. Kerrigan wasn't feeling at all optimistic about relationships, and right now she just wanted to be left alone.

***

A few hours later, Kerrigan was looking through the cabinets in the kitchen, which were mostly bare. She did find a few canned goods of chicken noodle soup and tuna. She found a piece of scrap paper in one of the drawers, along with a pen, and she started to make a grocery list. She needed to start planning her meals. She was not eating healthy and she felt like changing that today. As she jotted a few items down on paper, she heard a soft knock at the door. She walked through the living room to open the door, and once again Meggie was waiting on the other side. This time, by herself.

"Well, hello again, sweet girl. Are you here all by yourself?" Kerrigan thought Nate, or Hallie, should be keeping a better eye on her given what had happened just twenty-four hours ago.

"Yes, I want some of my candy," Meggie answered and Kerrigan tried not to giggle out loud.

"Oh, you do? Well, *your* candy is in my kitchen, waiting for you," Kerrigan said. "Let's go get it." Kerrigan closed the door and followed Meggie into the kitchen. She was wearing another little sundress, this one pale yellow and she had on flip flops to match. Kerrigan noticed her small toe nails were even painted yellow.

Kerrigan pulled out a chair from under the kitchen table and Meggie crawled up on it, staying on her knees to be able to reach the basket of candy which Kerrigan had on the middle of the table as her centerpiece. As Meggie rooted through the basket, Kerrigan asked her again about being there alone.

"Does your daddy, or Hallie, know you're here?" Kerrigan wondered if Nate had gotten called into work and

Hallie was supposed to be watching her for him.

"No. He is in the shower. Can I have the Starburst?"

"Yes, but just one, and then we are going to walk back to your house before your daddy realizes you are missing." Kerrigan smiled at Meggie, those sweet freckled-cheeks made her giggle.

"I want a red one," Meggie said, as Kerrigan peeled the paper off of the tiny cherry-red square of chewy candy and handed it to her. "Chew very carefully, and then we will leave."

Kerrigan watched Meggie cautiously chew, and then the two of them walked over to Nate's house together. When they reached the door, Kerrigan suggested to Meggie, "We should probably knock first."

Meggie giggled. "This is my daddy's house, I don't have to knock first." And then Kerrigan followed her inside. "Daddy, I'm home!" Meggie yelled and Kerrigan smiled. *This child is a delight*, she thought to herself, as she spotted Nate coming down the hallway, wearing only a blue towel wrapped around his waist.

"Oh, hi," he said to Kerrigan and looked down at Meggie. "I thought we were here alone. And why did you yell that you're home? Did you leave while I was in the shower?" Nate looked at Meggie, and then at Kerrigan. He didn't seem to appear the least bit embarrassed about being nearly naked, but Kerrigan was feeling uncomfortable. She didn't want to stare but *holy smokes* this man's broad chest, still somewhat wet from the shower, and his fit torso unwittingly attracted her eyes.

"I went to Kerrigan's to get my candy!" Meggie exclaimed. "Don't worry, daddy, she watched me chew and swallow the red Starburst." Both Nate and Kerrigan looked at each other and smiled.

"Okay, well that's good, but I don't want you running out of this house without telling me again, you hear me?"

"I only went to Kerrigan's," Meggie stated.

"It doesn't matter. I need to know. Your mother would not like me very much if I lost you." Nate tried not to crack a smile at his little girl.

"She doesn't like you very much anyway, daddy." The bluntness of a child could sometimes be comical, but this time Kerrigan felt sad knowing a little girl had to be a witness to parents who did not get along.

"Meggie, she does too like me." Nate defended himself.

"Not as much as she likes Jenny," Meggie replied, and Kerrigan was confused but chalked up the comment to Meggie only being four. Maybe Nate would explain, she thought, but he didn't. He just excused himself to go get dressed, but not before telling Kerrigan not to leave. She assumed he wanted her to keep an eye on Meggie for a few minutes and so she did.

It was only five minutes, but Meggie had quickly convinced Kerrigan into playing a game of Chutes and Ladders. Kerrigan was seated on the floor in front of the couch with her legs under the coffee table and Meggie was kneeling beside her when Nate returned. He was wearing baggy, khaki cargo shorts and a plain red t-shirt and his feet were bare.

"Oh good, she talked you into playing," Nate winked at Kerrigan and Meggie beamed. She had a new friend, someone to eat candy with and play her favorite board game with.

"I loved this game as a kid," Kerrigan said as she watched Meggie spin the arrow and begin to count her steps on the board.

"I'll bet you were a cute kid, Fred," Nate said, sitting down on the couch behind them and Kerrigan blushed. There she sat in her elastic shirts, oversized t-shirt and flip flops. She could feel her stomach rolls mesh together like an accordion and she knew her boobs looked saggy. Bra or not, she still had full breasts from being pregnant and later breast feeding Piper for five weeks. Except for the tan, which was beginning to look evident on her skin after a week of living on the beach, Kerrigan felt self conscious being in the room with Nate, in his house.

Those uncomfortable thoughts quickly shifted to ease when Meggie brought Kerrigan's attention back to the game. A half an hour of playing and sharing casual conversation with both Nate and Meggie went by, and Kerrigan was truly enjoying herself.

"Daddy, I know what we can do next with Kerrigan," Meggie said, as her face lit up with what she thought was a perfect idea. "She can cook and eat skettie with us!"

"What's skettie?" Kerrigan asked, hoping she could get out of this invitation. She didn't want to overstay her welcome.

"Spaghetti," Nate explained. "Will you stay?"

"I really should get going," Kerrigan said, and Meggie immediately responded with, "Please stay!"

"Oh come on, Fred," Nate teased her. "If you have no other plans, you need to join us." Meggie wrapped her arms around Kerrigan's neck and squeezed her tight until she surrendered and agreed to stay for dinner.

***

Kerrigan was not much help in the kitchen because she continued to give in to Meggie's pleas to play as Nate cooked. While they were eating dinner, the conversation revolved around Meggie. Kerrigan had fallen in love with that little girl today. Being with her made her feel alive again. Nate was watching the two of them play together while he was in the kitchen, and he too recognized their bond. His little girl seemed good for Kerrigan. Whatever was paining her since she arrived in Orange Beach, now appeared to be far from her thoughts.

Forty minutes after dinner was eaten and the dishes were done, with Kerrigan's help this time, Meggie came into the kitchen where Nate and Kerrigan were standing at the counter talking. She was carrying her small pink backpack and her pink blanket to match. Her head was hanging low when Nate stepped over toward her, took the backpack and set it down on the floor at their feet, and then he swooped her up into his arms. "Hey Meg, no tears, the week will go fast and you can come back again, okay?" Kerrigan now realized it was time for Meggie to go back with her mother, to spend the weekdays with her as she only spent the weekends with her father.

"But, daddy, I didn't get the whole weekend with you because I choked and then mommy made me come back home with her last night." Meggie was on the verge of crying as Nate did his best to console her.

"I know, and because that happened I am going to ask mommy if I can have you an extra night next weekend. How does Friday, Saturday, and Sunday night sound to you?"

"Yay! I want to, daddy, so please make mommy say yes!" Meggie's tears were gone and Nate had succeeded at cheering her up. Kerrigan still did not know their family's story, but she was quick to put the missing pieces together in her mind when Meggie's mother and a woman named Jenny showed up to take Meggie home with them.

A short, petite and extremely fit, blonde-haired woman walked into Nate's beach house first. Her hair was poker straight and ended halfway down her back. Her body looked amazing and her facial features were just beautiful. She looked like she could have graced the cover of a magazine. She wore short, black spandex shorts, which Kerrigan thought could have passed as boyshorts underwear, and a tight peach tank top, layered with a white tank top underneath. Jenny, her friend who followed behind her, also had blonde hair but her style was cropped short, only about two or three inches long all over her head. She stood a little bit taller than Meggie's mother and carried a thicker body, equally as toned. Kerrigan suddenly felt like a ball of blubber compared to them all.

"All ready to go, Meggie Mouse?" she asked as Meggie immediately clung to Kerrigan and Nate watched her. They all were watching, and Kerrigan suddenly felt like a misfit. She was just a neighbor, a new neighbor, a temporary neighbor, on the beach for the summer.

"I want to stay here with my new friend, her name is Kerrigan," Meggie whined as Kerrigan tried to smile at this woman whose child didn't want to go home with her. Nate then interjected to ease the awkwardness in the room. "This is Kerrigan, our new neighbor, she's staying in MJ's beach house for the summer. She saved our daughter from choking last night."

Meggie's mother immediately walked over to Kerrigan. She reached out to her with her hands and grabbed both of Kerrigan's. "You're the one? Oh my God, thank you for saving my little girl." Kerrigan felt uncomfortable with this woman's hands on hers, but she tried not to show it.

"You're welcome. Your little girl is a gem." Kerrigan didn't know what else to say, and again Nate spoke.

"Kerrigan, this is my ex-wife, Bryn and her girlfriend, Jenny," Nate said, watching Kerrigan's eyes widen. It all made sense now.

The three of them shared a few more minutes of small talk while Meggie warmed up to the idea of going back home with her mom and Jenny. It had to be difficult for a four-year-old to adjust to switching homes, Kerrigan kept thinking as the three of them walked out the door, after she promised Meggie she would see her on Friday night. Bryn agreed to Nate's idea to keep their daughter an extra night next weekend. In fact, she and her girlfriend both seemed pleased and discussed the possibility of going out of town, right there in front of the rest of them.

When they left, Nate closed the door and Kerrigan stood up and spoke first this time. "Wow, I had no idea. I mean, I assumed Meggie's chatter about her mom's friend, Jenny was just a *friend* named Jenny." Kerrigan felt like a worldly person, she socialized with gay people in college and she had gay friends back in Baltimore. She understands a person's sexual preference is their own business, but standing there trying to fathom a woman leaving a man like Nate for another woman was inconceivable to her at the moment. *How could she go from being attracted to a manly man like Nate, to a woman?*

"Nope, Jenny is more than a friend to the woman I used to call my wife," Nate answered as he walked through the living room and into the kitchen. "Sit down, I will get us some wine, and tell you the story."

Kerrigan sat down on the couch and Nate joined her with two empty glasses and a chilled bottle of red wine in his hands. He set the glasses down on his coffee table and poured the wine. It has been a long time since Kerrigan had a drink, since before she had gotten pregnant with Piper. She enjoyed wine and freely accepted the glass Nate handed to her. She pushed the idea out of her mind how this was beginning to feel like a date. An afternoon which started out as a playdate had now turned into being alone with this man. And drinking wine.

"My wife and I were married for five years," Nate said as Kerrigan thought of Keith and the two of them also being married for five years. "And Jenny has always been a part of the picture. They were friends. I had no clue there could have been more going on between them. I never paid attention to how it may have been too much the way they sat close, hung on each other, touched each other, or hugged, or whatever. Girls are close, men know that." Nate stopped talking to take a long swig of his wine and Kerrigan did the same. She felt like she was going to need it in order to hear the rest of the story.

"One night, six months ago now, I came home from working late and I walked in on the two of them on my couch." Nate explained, as Kerrigan blurted out, "Oh my God…"

"They weren't naked, thank God, because Meggie was in the house sleeping at the time. But, they were in each other's arms. My wife's shirt was unbuttoned, her bra was undone, and Jenny's pants were halfway off. They never even heard me come in. I just stood there watching two women, one of them being my wife, in the middle of some serious foreplay."

Kerrigan blushed at the thought of it and Nate finished off the wine in his glass and asked her if she too wanted a refill. Kerrigan nodded her head as he poured more wine into their glasses. "I don't know what to say," she said, "It sounds like a scene from a movie."

"No, it was real," Nate responded, "and so was the heartache."

"I'm sorry," Kerrigan said, becoming more serious. "I cannot imagine your pain, I mean, you two share a child, a beautiful little girl who deserves a stable home life."

"I struggled with that for a long while, and I still have a hard time with it, but I'm moving on for Meggie's sake," Nate said. "I mean, we all get along, we always have. As I said, Jenny has been a part of our lives, our family. I just never realized she was such a huge part of my marriage and would be the one who would end up destroying it."

"Were they sleeping together while you two were married?" The wine obviously made Kerrigan a little bolder with her questions.

"Bryn says not. She says this was a shock to the two of them as well. They fought their feelings, only talking about it before acting on anything. But, when they gave in, they decided there was no turning back. They want to be together, so I'm the odd man out. I'm the guy whose wife would rather sleep with a woman." The wine had already gotten to Nate as well.

"I can't believe it, and I am sorry for your pain," Kerrigan said as she sipped more wine.

"Thank you. It not easy, but Meggie seems to be adjusting better than we all expected. Kids do that, you know." Suddenly, Kerrigan felt pained. No, she didn't know, and she wouldn't know, because Piper was lost to her as a five-week-old baby. She would not grow to become a little girl because she was dead. Kerrigan felt chilled as she placed her empty wine glass down on the coffee table in front of her. It was back. The memory. The torment. That truth, that sadness, had not crossed her mind all day. But, now, it had.

"Are you okay? Did I say something wrong?" Nate asked, reading her body language.

"I'm fine, I just really need to get back to my place," Kerrigan said, starting to stand up, and Nate stopped her. He gently put his hand on her forearm and spoke. "Please, stay. It's not easy to tell someone what hurts so badly, what you may have buried inside of you, but sometimes it's the only way to deal with it…and try to move on."

Kerrigan wanted to pull away from him. She wanted to run out of his door and never look back. She wanted to avoid this course she was on. It was a risk. It could mean more pain. But, it could also mean something good. She was scared and she allowed her fear to take over, and she did pull away from him, and walked quickly over to the door.

She kept her back to him as her hand reached for the door handle. She stood there and she could feel the tears beginning to fill her eyes and teeter on her long, dark eyelashes. And Nate saw them too as she turned around to look back at him. He was still sitting on the couch. He thought she was going to run again and he knew he had no other choice other than to allow her to, but that's when she walked slowly back over to the couch and sat down beside him and stayed.

    She was silent for a long time before she spoke with tears beginning to trickle from both of her eyes and down her face. Nate wanted to take his fingers and wipe them away, wash away her pain, but he didn't. He was so afraid he would scare her off, so he just sat close to her and listened.

Chapter 7

Kerrigan was trembling when she explained to him how she found her baby in her crib, lifeless. Nate was deeply moved, imagining the terrifying moment happening to him with his own little girl. And he was touched to his very core, moved to having tears in his own eyes because he cared about this woman, new to the beach and now to his – and Meggie's – life.

Before Kerrigan could continue speaking, to finish the rest of the story about her marriage being over, and her best friend being lost to her as well, she began crying and she could not stop. This was the first time she had told anyone what happened. Keith had made the phone calls when they lost Piper. She never said the words out loud to anyone, until now. She started to sob, bent forward on the couch beside Nate, with her face in her hands. He softly placed his hands on her shoulders, lifted her upright, turned her toward him with his strong arms, his gentle hands, and he pulled her close. She fell against his chest and she stayed there for a very long time, crying and finally allowing herself to be comforted by someone. She had not allowed anybody in. Not Keith or Gail or anyone who came to her to offer their sympathy, their help, their open arms. Tonight, that had changed for her.

In Nate's arms, she felt swept away. She felt like the waves of the ocean water she had been watching for days from her deck. The waves come in and they sweep away anything in their path and then they wash back out to sea, farther and farther away until they're gone. That is how Kerrigan felt in this man's arms. He was taking her pain, embracing it with her, and then helping her wash it away, far away. Like the waves though, Kerrigan knew the pain would come back. But, she now believed her next wave of sadness just might be a little more bearable with Nate there to comfort her.

When she came to that realization, she slowly pulled her body out of his embrace. He felt bold enough this time to take her face into his hands and use his fingers to wipe the tears off of her face. She allowed him to, and smiled at him.

"Thank you for being here for me. I've been drowning in my grief and feeling pretty damn alone these days," Kerrigan confessed.

"Why did you run? Isn't there anyone back home who you could have turned to?" Nate paused, and then he asked her. "What about your husband?" He had never seen her wear a wedding ring, but since her baby had only been gone for several weeks, he assumed a woman like Kerrigan had to be married.

"My husband is now sharing our home and our bed with my best friend," Kerrigan replied, without shedding a tear. It was easier for her to tell this next story. Nate sat there in silence, taking it all in, just as Kerrigan had with his story about his lesbian wife. After she finished explaining the entire saga about Gail Boyd always carrying a torch for her first lover, and how Keith never stopped longing for her either, Nate looked disgusted.

"Then they deserve each other," he said, shaking his head. "Don't look back on that son of bitch without a backbone or a worthy set of balls."

Kerrigan giggled and said aloud, "That's the plan." And then she looked forlorn again. "Losing Piper is just too much. I can handle my failed marriage, but I cannot handle my baby dying." Nate took her hand in his.

"Of course you feel like you cannot handle it. Who in the hell is strong enough for such a sickening pain? I may look big and strong to you, but let me tell you something. You, Kerrigan Fred, have a strength I admire because I now know you are carrying something in your heart that I could never handle. Ever." Of course Nate was imagining losing Meggie and no parent ever wants to see their worst nightmare of losing a child come true. It was devastating and it seemed unmanageable, but what other choice did Kerrigan have?

"First, my last name is Ross, not Fred," she smiled at him, having realized they never shared their last names. She didn't know his either. "Second, I don't feel like I'm handling anything, or at least I haven't until you came along, especially tonight. And finally, I don't know your last name."

Nate returned a smile to her. "First, I like Fred better for you. Second, I want to be here for you, not just tonight, but for as long as you need me. And last, it's Stein."

"Nate Stein," Kerrigan said aloud. "Sounds masculine." She giggled at him and he joined her as they both remembered her teasing him when they first met, just days ago in the sand.

It did not seem like only recently since they met, not to either of them, as they sat close to each other on the couch and felt a connection which had almost instantaneously brought them both back to life. For Nate, the longing for his wife and the loneliness he felt for many months had finally began to dissipate. For Kerrigan, she just did not feel as sad or as alone. She even liked the surprise tingly feeling she had running through her body as she sat there thinking of Nate

Stein as a man. She caught herself wondering what it might feel like if he would press his lips to hers and kiss her, and before she had the chance to tell herself to chase that thought right out of her mind because *it's too soon*, because *he may not even reciprocate those feelings for her*, she watched him lean his body toward hers. He again could read her mind. And he was about to reassure her that he did reciprocate the same feelings she had stirring inside of her. In fact, he had those feelings before she did. He felt his insides stir and his heart open up for her the night he found her crying in the dark on the couch in her beach house. He wanted to hold her in his arms then and never let go of her.

She was the first woman he had kissed since his wife left him, so when he met his lips with hers, there was a mounting desire, there was an eagerness to the feel of his lips on hers, his tongue finding its way around hers and Kerrigan responded with a feeling comparable to desperation. She wanted this. She wanted him. But, more than anything, this was the first time, other than trying to run on the beach, she had found a way to forget. Even if it was only going to last for a little while, even if the pain and the memory were only going to subside temporarily. Kerrigan wanted to seize the feeling and this moment. She wanted to feel desired, she wanted to feel ecstasy with this man. They kissed for what seemed like an eternity and their passion for each other escalated to a new level when Nate reached up inside of her shirt and touched her breast through her bra. He slipped his hand inside of one of the cups and he caressed her nipple. He wanted to see her, too. So he began to lift up her shirt. Kerrigan suddenly felt self conscious. Here she was about to become intimate with a man whose former wife had a body that just wouldn't quit – so fit, so fabulous, so shapely. Kerrigan knew she was fat, she still had baby weight on her already full body. Nate sensed she was pulling away from him and he assumed she was not ready to be with him yet. "I'm sorry, I just got carried away, I'm insanely turned on by you right now. I want to see, and feel, your body."

"Nate, I'm fat and I just met your ex-wife who doesn't have an iota of body fat anywhere!" Kerrigan wanted to laugh, but she felt embarrassed now.

"Yeah, my ex-wife is hot," Nate stated, and Kerrigan felt even more uncomfortable, "but that's not everything to me anymore," he continued. "Bryn left me, she broke my heart, split up our family, and now everything about her is tarnished in my eyes. You are a woman to me, Kerrigan. I see your full figure and I also see a beautiful woman, inside and out. You're real. You make me laugh, and you obviously already adore my daughter. You're a woman I want to get to know better. Let me touch you, all of you…" Nate began to reach under her shirt again and she let him slip it over her head and off of her. Then, she allowed her desire for him to overtake how self conscious she felt as she reached behind her back and undid the clasp on her bra. Her breasts were now free as Nate reached for them. He was fondling her nipples when she took his face into her hands and pulled him toward her chest. He took his time and she had never felt so special. He was attentive. That is not what she was used to. Keith wanted to get to the part where he was inside of her, thrusting toward his climax. The attention Nate was giving her now made Kerrigan forget her stomach rolls and her sagging breasts. She made the move to take off his shirt and then she undid the button and zipper on his shorts. When she reached into his underwear, he sprang up into her hand. This big, strong man had a manhood to match. Kerrigan was taken by surprise as he stood up and allowed his pants and underwear to fall to the floor in front of the couch. Then he took her by the hand and led her into his bedroom. The sheets needed to be pulled back, but they didn't take the time for that. He sat down on the end of the bed as she stood in front of him. He kissed her breasts hard and aggressively and then he made his way down to the waistband of her shorts. He pulled them down and off quickly and her underwear went with them. They were just a pair of stretched-out, cotton ones, nothing lacy or sexy, so Kerrigan was relieved to see them on the floor at her feet as she stood naked in front of him. He found her with his fingers and slipped one up inside of her. She moaned, still standing, as he touched her deep inside and simultaneously found her clitoris with his thumb. This man's fingers were long, huge and incredibly satisfying as he touched her. This continued and she let it happen, she lost herself in how this made her feel. She felt her legs become shaky as he recognized she was close, so he dropped to his knees on the floor in front of her and carried on, touching her, making her come closer and closer. She moaned aloud, again and again and again, before finally she came and when she did he had pulled his fingers out and away from her and met her with his tongue and his lips. And God they both wanted more. She fell back onto the bed with him on top of her and he immediately made his way inside of her, filling her like no man had before, and his thrusts made them both cry out with pleasure. When he let himself go inside of her, he pulled her into his arms and held her close. His body meshed against hers. Her heart beating in sync with his. It had not been just about sex for either one of them.

Chapter 8

Kerrigan woke up in Nate's arms. He was still asleep when she opened her eyes and felt him as close to her as he was when she closed her eyes last night. She laid there for a few minutes, thinking how she's not *that kind of girl*. She'd never had a one night stand or even a fling. She wondered if the two of them were just lonely and hurting last night. She prepared herself for things to be different this morning, but *it sure was amazing to be with this man, to take the weight off of my mind for awhile.*

Just as she was contemplating slipping out of his arms and out of the bed to retrieve her clothes, still on the floor since last night, Nate's alarm clock sounded on the nightstand beside the bed. He jumped in his sleep and stretched out his arm to hit the snooze button. He never opened his eyes, until he quickly realized she was there. "Well good morning, Fred," he said, wrapping both of his arms around Kerrigan and squeezing her with his long arms and large hands. This man actually made Kerrigan feel small at times. She giggled and replied, "Is this your first time waking up next to a Fred?"

"First and last, I hope," Nate replied kissing her full on the mouth and she responded as their movement pulled the sheet away from her body. It was light in his bedroom now and she felt self conscious being naked in front of him again. She started to pull the sheet back up and over her stomach and chest when she looked at his tight chest. He didn't have a torso comparable to a six pack, but his muscles were firm and tight. She stopped staring and covered herself with the sheet.

"I should tell you that I prefer a full-figured woman," Nate said, sensing how she was feeling as she covered her body. Kerrigan rolled her eyes at him, "No man thinks that way, and full-figured is a nice way of saying fat."

"Love yourself, Kerrigan and if you need to make changes to your body in order to, then do it. I have seen your drive when you speed walk down the beach and when you run. Keep it up and get into shape to feel better or look better in your eyes, but in my eyes last night and again right now, you are hot and sexy and I need to get out of this bed and get ready for work before I let you get me all worked up again." Kerrigan smiled at him and thanked him with a kiss on the lips.

As he slipped out of bed, she watched him and she tried not to go there in her mind. She tried not to think those words, but she did anyway. *I could get used to this. To him.*

***

While Nate was taking a shower, Kerrigan put yesterday's clothes back on. She wanted to go back to her beach house for a shower and some clean clothes, but she waited to tell Nate goodbye.

She was in the kitchen, thinking about making him a quick breakfast, but she didn't know what he liked or if he was even a breakfast person. And that's when he walked in, dressed in jeans, a burgundy polo shirt, his brown boat shoes, and a brown belt with his police badge clipped to it. "Where's your uniform, officer?" Kerrigan asked him. "Is it an undercover day for you?"

Nate smiled at her, "I would like to be under the covers all day with you." She giggled and she wondered if they would end up there again. He walked to the refrigerator and took out a protein shake and then grabbed an apple out of the fruit basket on the counter. "I'm taking breakfast to-go today, but you stay and help yourself to whatever looks good." Nate walked toward her and kissed her gently on the lips.

"Thank you, but I will leave when you do," she said, returning his kiss and smelling the fresh cologne on his neck.

"Okay, be safe going home," he teased, regarding her short walk across the sand, as he began to walk out the door.

"Have a good day, Nate," Kerrigan said, beginning to follow him out the door so he could lock it. And that's when he turned to her.

"I will, because last night was wonderful. Thank you for letting me in. Thank you for sharing your grief," he spoke softly to her and then he pulled her into his arms in front of the closed door. He held her for a moment before she pulled out of his arms and whispered, "Thank you for being there for me."

As Nate walked in the sand and up to the road where his squad car was parked next to Kerrigan's old jeep, she walked in the opposite direction toward her beach house. She felt funny coming home from being with a man last night, and she felt a little uneasy passing Hallie's house. She picked up her pace, hoping she was still asleep or too busy at the moment to look out the window and spot her, and that is when her nosy neighbor hollered from her open kitchen window. "Good morning, Kerrigan!"

Kerrigan stopped in her tracks, focused on the face in the open window for a brief moment as she gave Hallie an awkward wave of her hand high in the air and then she began walking again and didn't look back until she reached her deck, her door, and she closed it swiftly behind her before she breathed again. *Busted.*

***

Kerrigan knew it was just a matter of time, and shortly after lunch Hallie popped in. She never knocked, but Kerrigan had actually gotten used to Hallie barging in after only one week of living next door to her. Kerrigan had just returned from the grocery store. Yesterday, she was making the grocery list when Meggie came over, and so much had happened since then. It felt good to be that close to Nate, talking openly and honestly, and making love, but again Kerrigan was not entirely sure about it now. Or about him. They are not in a relationship, but could they be? Did she want to be? Did he? And was it wise to get so close to Meggie? *Too late for that.*

"Come on in, Hallie," Kerrigan said with a sarcastic tone as Hallie was already inside, wearing a taupe-colored muu-muu today with her trademark Birkenstocks, and pulling out a chair by the table where Kerrigan was unpacking her bags of groceries.

"How are you, honey? You look a little different since the last time I saw you." Hallie had a mischievous look about her and Kerrigan blushed. "Oh hush, nothing is different about me."

"You can tell an old lady, you know. These days the most action I get is from reading a stack of steamy romance novels." Hallie laughed and coughed at the same time.

"I had dinner with Nate and Meggie last night," she confessed. "It was nice. He's a good cook."

"Is he good at anything else?" Hallie asked, desperately wanting to hear more.

"He's a good dad. He told me his ex-wife left him because she chose to make a life with another woman." Her best friend. Kerrigan still could not believe that story.

"Yes, I still think she will regret her choice someday. A man like Nate is hard to find." Hallie meant those words. She adored Nate and she wanted to see him happy. She wanted to see Kerrigan happy, too. It worried her to see such a young woman consumed with sadness.

Kerrigan just smiled at Hallie because she knew she had a soft spot in her heart for Nate and his little girl. After a few minutes of silence as Kerrigan kept herself busy putting away a few things in her kitchen, Hallie spoke again. "So when are you going to admit to me that you spent the night with him last night?" It was just like Hallie to blurt out exactly what she was thinking, when she was thinking it, without any couth, Kerrigan thought as her eyes widened and her cheeks flushed.

"Who said I spent the night with him?" Kerrigan was not ready for this. This woman was prying and acting overprotective and, well, like a mother. Kerrigan never had a real mother. Dottie Boyd never got too personal. She didn't even really know what was going on with her biological daughter half the time, and maybe that was a good thing.

"I have nothing better to do sometimes than to look out my window. It's not terribly busy out here on this end of the beach, honey. I do see when people walk by at lunchtime and never walk back until the next morning, still wearing the same clothes as the day before." Hallie said, sounding as if her voice was suppressing another cough. She cleared her throat as Kerrigan looked at her and then decided to sit down at the table with her.

"First of all, I just want to say I'm not *that kind of girl*," Kerrigan said, feeling awkward and making fleeting eye contact between Hallie and the candy basket from Meggie sitting on the center of the table. "I opened up to him, or more like I fell apart about what brought me here, to the beach, this summer. He's been through an ordeal with Bryn and he's faced that pain. I'm still in pain and he reached out to me. He's trying to help me get through it, I guess, or just be there for me."

"You don't have to tell me what it is, Kerrigan," Hallie told her, "but do know that I feel great relief knowing you have found someone to talk to. We can't grieve alone, it takes us down too far." Hallie patted Kerrigan's hand on top of the table as she spoke to her.

Kerrigan would not look at her. She looked down at their hands together on top of the table and she could feel the tears in her eyes welling up and beginning to spill over. "I lost my five-week-old baby girl to SIDS," the tears continued to fall, but this time Kerrigan's voice was strong, "and my husband turned to my best friend for comfort – and just to be clear my best friend is a whore." Kerrigan spelled it all out in one long sentence, as Hallie swallowed hard.

"Oh dear God, I am so sorry." Hallie sat there for a moment, staring down at her lap, shaking her head back and forth. She had suspected Kerrigan's pain stemmed from something bad, but she never expected this. "Your baby. God needs to see that sometimes it's just too much."

"I know, Hallie," Kerrigan said, squeezing her hand this time as she thought of her losing all three of her daughters at once. Hallie had tears in her eyes when she looked up from her lap. She retrieved a tissue from inside of her dress, tucked into her bra. She opened it and blew her nose hard and loud before wadding up that tissue and stuffing it back in between her boobs. Kerrigan thought of that gesture as *gross*, but she had quickly come to care about this old woman and her quirks.

"I should apologize for assuming you and Nate rocked the house over there last night," Hallie said as Kerrigan felt like giggling inside. "I am happy to know he has been a comfort to you, a friend to you."

"He's an amazing lover, too, Hallie." Kerrigan could not believe she said those words, but *what the hell* they needed to break this solemn mood in her kitchen. After Hallie howled with laughter, which transitioned into a coughing spell that prompted Kerrigan to get up and fill a glass of iced water for her, she finally was able to respond to Kerrigan's comment.

"Good for you!" she applauded her. "Sometimes we just have to say fuck it, let it all go, and do something without even thinking about it."

"That's exactly what I did last night," Kerrigan replied, "and the funny thing is the old me would have regretted it, but I don't. *Enjoy the moment* is going to be my new theme for this summer. I feel like I need those moments to get through my loss, whether it's a long walk on the beach or being with Nate." Kerrigan didn't want to depend on him, and she already told herself – and now Hallie – that she would just be taking things as they come with no expectations.

"I hear you, honey…and I want you to know something. When I lost my girls, I had those people in my life who offered support or anything else they could do or get for me. Those kinds of people would say to me, 'it's going to be okay,' and I used to think, what the hell is *okay*? I lost my whole world so what could ever be *okay* again? Well, with time, my life is okay, but what makes it okay is seizing those moments like we just talked about. Those moments will see you through." And that was all Hallie said as she hoped neither one of her neighbors on either side of her would end up with a broken heart by summer's end. She wanted them both to be better than okay.

***

Kerrigan found herself with a new energy as she cleaned the beach house, prepared and cooked a pot of vegetable beef soup on the stove top, and held on tight to the positive vibes flowing through her body. About an hour before dinner time, she searched MJ's cabinets and found the perfect sized bowl with a lid on it for which she added some soup and then walked over to Hallie's with it.

She knocked twice before she heard Hallie coming toward the closed door. When she opened it, she smiled at Kerrigan as she handed her the bowl and asked her if she had prepared anything for dinner yet. "Does this mean you didn't have your fill of me this morning, preaching about nothing at all to you?" Hallie asked, grateful to get the soup.

"I wouldn't say *nothing at all*," Kerrigan responded. "Your words have helped me more than you know and this is my way of saying thank you. I hope you like vegetable beef soup. I know it's eighty-five degrees today but if you're like me, you can always eat a bowl of soup."

"I'm like you," Hallie said, smiling. Kerrigan left after they chatted at the door for a few additional minutes. Hallie seemed tired to her, and her coughing appeared more consistent, so she wanted to let her rest.

When Kerrigan walked back into her kitchen, she wondered if she should share some soup with Nate, too. Maybe it was too much to be standing at his door with his dinner the night after they were intimate. She didn't want to appear clingy or needy or God forbid, desperate. She decided against that idea and an hour later she spooned two full ladles of soup into a bowl for herself. Just as she sat down at her table in the kitchen, she heard a knock.

She walked over to the door, thinking Hallie always barges in and she felt her insides flutter, knowing there was a very good chance it's Nate.

"Something smells so good coming from this house, I seriously could smell it all the way down to mine," Nate was still in his work clothes, police badge and all, smiling from ear to ear at Kerrigan.

"You must have one hell of a sniffer," she teased as she stepped back from the door and he came inside.

"It's been awhile since I've heard that from a woman," Nate replied and Kerrigan laughed out loud, and added, "Well, that too," as Nate pulled her close and kissed her hard on the mouth. She felt incredibly swept away with him, again. Kerrigan slowly pulled back and tried to take in a breath.

"Let me feed you tonight," she said as they both went into the kitchen and she filled a second bowl of soup and placed it on the table in front of him.

"I should have brought some wine," Nate said as he tasted and complimented her on the homemade soup.

"I picked up a bottle at the grocery store today," she said, and he suggested, "save it for later."

And later, Nate was still at her house. They ate, talked, cleaned up their dishes, and shared some wine when they ended up on the couch in the living room. Neither one of them spoke about what could be happening between them. It was too soon to speculate or have any great hopes, they both knew that, but it wasn't too soon to seize the moment, like Hallie said, and they both held tight to another night together which began on her couch and ended with explosive passion in her bed this time.

Chapter 9

Kerrigan was sitting in the nursery, in the rocking chair near the crib. She had just fed her baby and started to rock her back to sleep. Only the nightlight plugged into the wall socket lit the room. The sight of Piper's full cheeks, her tiny hands with long fingers, and the sound of her breathing as she held her close made Kerrigan feel so grateful to God for this chance to be a mother.

Heartless

Kerrigan sat up straight after waking up with a jolt, and realized she had been dreaming about her baby. She seemed so real, so alive. Kerrigan had Piper's yellow blanket wadded up on top of her pillow. She reached for it, held it, and brought it close to her face as the tears from her eyes fell onto it. One dream, exactly like that, could bring it all back too fast, too harshly. Maybe someday the pain would not feel so raw, but right now, for Kerrigan, it just hurt too much.

The moment Piper was born remained so vivid in her mind as Kerrigan curled up alone in the dark, in the middle of the night, in the sleigh bed at the beach house and she thought back to that day.

Keith was panicked as he drove them too fast to the hospital in his small pick-up truck. "Are you sure you're not going to have the baby right here? Those contractions are coming closer and closer together." He slammed on his brakes to stop in time for the traffic light that had turned red in front of them. He was barely an inch away from the rear bumper of the car in front of them.

"Your chances of throwing me through the windshield are greater than me having this baby before we get to the hospital. Calm down, we will make it, the baby will wait."

Kerrigan rubbed her large, perfectly round belly as she felt another contraction begin and she tried to breathe. Her baby, their baby, was about to make an appearance. A grand entrance was more like it. It took five years to get to this point. Five difficult years after getting pregnant, miscarrying and then trying month after month to conceive. The doctors couldn't explain it, both Keith and Kerrigan were put through fertility tests and checked out fine. They just kept trying, but it consumed them, especially Kerrigan. She wanted a baby more than anything. Keith wanted his wife to get pregnant, but for him it had become more about seeing her get what she so desperately wanted, rather than it being his answered prayer.

At first he was totally against it, it was *too expensive and who's to say it will even take*, but Kerrigan insisted and with some assistance from their insurance and a loan from the bank, they tried in vitro fertilization and became pregnant on the first attempt.

Those thirty-eight weeks passed quickly and it had been an easy, typical pregnancy. And when her water broke two weeks before their baby's due date, Kerrigan wasn't scared. She was excited. She was eager to meet her baby, the baby she and Keith had not known in advance if it was a boy or a girl.

And when that baby girl was placed in her arms, Kerrigan felt for the first time in her life what it meant to love unconditionally. This baby had her heart and Kerrigan had never felt more fulfilled. Keith cried when he held Piper Rose for the first time. He had no idea a baby, a new life, could make him feel that way, and he expressed as much to his wife. "She's amazing, and she wouldn't be here if it weren't for you," he said, sincerely, as Kerrigan reached for his hand when he sat beside her hospital bed and held their baby.

They were going to make it. The years of trying and the stress it put on their marriage dissipated that day because they had gotten their miracle.

And then, five weeks later, they lost her and it became inevitable they would also lose each other.

When they walked back into their house together after Piper's funeral, they weren't alone. Gail followed them in her vehicle and into their house. Kerrigan sat down on the couch in the living room, still in tears from the day's horrific events, and she ignored both of them when they emerged from the kitchen and offered her a glass of iced water, and Gail told her she needed to eat or drink something.

The glass sat untouched on the coffee table in front of her. When Keith gave up and walked to the back of the house, into their bedroom, Gail sat down close to Kerrigan. She didn't speak, she just opened her arms and Kerrigan willingly fell into them. Sometimes no words needed to be spoken.

Gail was there for Kerrigan that day, and for many other days in their lives together. And today, as the sun came up and Kerrigan was still lying in her bed awake, she continued to think of Gail and how much she still loved her. Despite everything.

It was the first time she did this since she arrived at the beach house almost two weeks ago, but Kerrigan thought maybe it was time. She got out of bed, walked over to the chest of drawers by the window and opened the top drawer to retrieve her cell phone. The battery was only twenty percent when Kerrigan powered on the phone.

She had eighteen text messages waiting for her. More than half of them were from friends, neighbors, and coworkers who were offering their condolences or just checking on her. And then three of those messages were from Keith.

Let me know where you are and if you're okay! ...It's wrong to run, Kerrigan. ...I know our marriage is over, but we still have things to talk about. The last message caught her attention.

He knew *their marriage was over*. Of course he did. At least that is what Gail Boyd had most likely been pumping into his mind, Kerrigan thought. She wished she didn't love her so much. She wanted to hate her. Who moves in on her best friend's husband, and especially while she and Keith were so consumed with grief? Kerrigan saw Keith initiate that kiss. She knew he still loved her, but she also saw Gail's response. Gail had been waiting for Keith to come back to her for a very long time.

It was not even about her marriage anymore. Kerrigan didn't want Keith back. She realized now how much their relationship was lacking. They were the closest of friends, but their relationship never should have gone any further. There was no spark, there was no desire. It felt forced when they were intimate and Kerrigan realized that now. Even before they tried to conceive a baby, they never knew passion. Not like Kerrigan has experienced with Nate. And obviously not like Keith shared with Gail.

Two texts were from *her*. Kerrigan used to light up when she saw Gail's name on her phone or computer. Texts and emails from her were a part of their daily routine. They checked in with each other constantly. They were friends, they were as close as sisters. And it pained Kerrigan now, knowing it had come to this.

She read both texts. *You need to talk to us.* That was the first one, and it made Kerrigan angry. *Us?* Was that Gail's way of stressing the obvious to Kerrigan, how she was together with Keith? And the second one was worse. *I think it's time you take a long look at yourself, make a list of your faults, and apply some changes.*

"I need to take a long look at myself?" Kerrigan said aloud to herself while she stood on the area rug under the bed. She could not take it anymore.

She pressed reply on her touch screen phone. She typed the words *You are heartless*, but before she sent it, she canceled the message. Without another thought, she powered off her phone and threw it back into the drawer and slammed it shut. *She's not worth it to me anymore.*

Kerrigan tried to keep that mindset for the rest of the morning, but it was exhausting. She needed to let go of Gail, like she had already done with Keith. She needed to get back to focusing on dealing with her grief and trying to move on.

She was looking forward to seeing Meggie tonight. Friday night had come quickly. Nate invited Kerrigan to spend the weekend with them, but she reminded him how careful they needed to be. *No sleepovers.* Nate had whined and Kerrigan giggled when she told him, "I said no sleepovers, I didn't say no sex."

***

Kerrigan may as well have been having sex with Nate when Bryn walked in the front door of his beach house with Meggie, and sans Jenny this time. Kerrigan was sitting on the couch and laughing out loud at Nate standing before her, acting like a little boy, begging her to sleepover tonight. They both knew it would be difficult to explain to Meggie why Kerrigan was spending the night when she only lived one house down from them. After one knock, the door opened up and Kerrigan watched Meggie run to her daddy and he picked her up and squeezed her. As Kerrigan's eyes were on Meggie and Nate, Bryn's eyes were on her. *And if looks could kill...*

Kerrigan smiled at Bryn, and the ex-wife spoke first. "Kerrigan? I didn't expect to see you here again." Kerrigan was not sure what her response should be, so she played it safe. "Oh, well, I couldn't stay away knowing this sweet girl was going to be here tonight." Kerrigan opened her arms as Meggie fell into them and sat up on her lap after their close hug. Bryn didn't look overly thrilled about that either.

She just stood there, by the closed front door, still holding Meggie's suitcase, looking unhappy. And Nate seemed oblivious to the tone in her voice and her icy glances as he walked over to her and took the suitcase out of her hand.

"So I guess you have a little getaway planned with your girlfriend this weekend?" he asked her as she looked surprised. She probably had forgotten about talking to Jenny in front of them last week about *getting away.*

"Um, no, Jenny ended up having to work so we're not going anywhere. You're still dropping off Meggie on your way to work Monday morning, right?"

"Yes," Nate replied, looking excited about Meggie staying with him one extra night this weekend. "We have a lot of fun things planned for our long weekend, Meg." Meggie jumped off the couch and asked, "With Kerrigan, too?" And that seemed to be the burning question in the room. Bryn wanted to know the answer, for sure, and Kerrigan was wondering just how much she should be around this weekend.

"Sure," Nate replied to his daughter, "if she wants to." Bryn looked unnerved as she walked over to Meggie, asked for a kiss goodbye, and told her to have a fun weekend *with her daddy.*

When she left, Meggie walked back into her bedroom to put her suitcase away. And that is when Kerrigan spoke with her voice low. "Well, I guess someone didn't care to see me here again."

"What? Bryn? Oh she's fine. It's not like she knows…" Nate replied in typical male fashion. *Why do women always pick up on the drama and men never see it coming, or recognize it when it's right in front of them?*

"Oh, she knows, or she senses it at least!" Kerrigan replied, feeling completely sure.

"Who cares if she does?" Nate said, walking over to Kerrigan, pulling her up off of the couch by both of her hands in his. "She chose to play for the other team, and I'm finally choosing to get back into the game."

"A game? Is that what we're playing?" Kerrigan asked.

"I'm not sure if that was the right way to put it," Nate replied, still holding her hands, "because when I look at you, I see the rest of forever." Kerrigan's eyes widened. She heard him, she rehashed the words in her head for a split second, she comprehended, but she was taken aback by him, by what he just said to her. She didn't have a chance to respond as Meggie returned into the room, requesting to know what *the first fun thing on the list is going to be.*

***

They were roasting marshmallows at their bonfire on the beach. Hallie came out of her house for the fun, too. Meggie was standing close to the fire with Nate's assistance as she roasted one marshmallow at a time, offering them to Hallie, Kerrigan and her daddy. She ate her share, too. She looked happy, as any kid would be, while doing something fun, and Kerrigan found herself wondering if this was where she's supposed to be. Had her spur of the moment summer escape to this beach been for a reason? A reason more than to run, hide, and attempt to get away to clear her mind and try to heal? Kerrigan was afraid. Afraid to think too much, to feel too much.

"What's going through that head of yours?" Hallie asked, bringing Kerrigan out of her deep thoughts as Meggie and Nate went back up to the house to wash her sticky fingers.

"Oh nothing really, just trying to process my life, and where I go from here," Kerrigan sarcastically replied.

"It's only been a few weeks, you have all summer yet. Don't be so quick to dwell and analyze. Sometimes we just need to let things happen," Hallie advised.

"I hear you, Hallie, but I'm just so afraid of losing again," Kerrigan admitted, feeling like she could already be in too deep. Nate's words earlier had stunned her. She wished he never would have said anything about *forever*. *Nothing is forever*, and it is just *too damn soon* for Kerrigan to even think about it. When she stepped foot in the sand of Orange Beach, Alabama, she promised herself *one day at a time*.

***

Meggie kept Kerrigan busy the rest of the evening. At bedtime, Kerrigan helped her with her bath and her pajamas. She curled up in Meggie's twin bed with her, reading the storybook she had chosen and before Kerrigan read the last page, Meggie fell asleep. She stayed with her for a few more minutes, feeling Meggie snuggled up close to her and listening to her breath. Kerrigan already felt so much love for this little girl, and so much joy when she was with her. She felt torn as she slipped carefully out of bed and made sure Meggie was completely covered before she left the room.

Nate was waiting for her in the living room when she walked down the hallway. "You're great with her, thank you for helping out so much tonight," Nate said as Kerrigan stood behind the armchair, looking over at him sitting on the couch.

"Is that what I'm here for, to help out?" Kerrigan asked him.

"I don't know what you mean...I know I want you here and so does Meggie," Nate answered, knowing all too well how fragile this woman is. But, nothing had changed for him. He still wanted to help her, get to know her even better, and just be with her. He was falling in love with her. Or maybe he already did love her.

"I want to be here, too," Kerrigan said, "but I feel like if I allow myself to jump into this with both feet, I am risking pain again...and to be honest, I am not strong enough for more loss in my life." She remained standing behind the armchair as Nate stood up and walked over to her. In bare feet, he still towered over her. *Such a big, strong man,* Kerrigan thought, *why can't I let him be strong for me?*

"I don't want you to worry about something that may never happen," Nate said.

"What if I go back to Baltimore when this summer is

Heartless

over?" Kerrigan asked, surprising herself. Staying at MJ's beach house was only temporary. But the thought of returning home with no one to go home to didn't appeal to Kerrigan. She just couldn't help herself right now. She wondered if she and Nate were only caught up in something, a summer fling, and eventually they would move on and away from each other.

"Is that what you want to do?" Nate asked her.

"I want to enjoy the moment, but I'm not allowing myself to… because the people in my life, who I have loved and trusted, failed me." It was the first time she had admitted it to herself. She suddenly felt like running scared. But, giving up on Nate and on the start of something that could be beautiful, scared her more.

"This is what I like about you, Kerrigan Ross," Nate said, choosing his words carefully because he wanted to say *love*. "You are hurting and scared shitless about what could happen, but you are being honest with yourself and with me. All I can tell you is I am not your husband and I am not your best friend. I am a man who has been let down, too, and right now I don't want to think too much…because I have not been this happy in a very long time." He smiled at Kerrigan and she felt teary looking up at him. "So let's play a game…"

"A game?" Kerrigan asked him, wondering how this serious moment had suddenly turned into *a game*.

"All summer long I want you to play *savor* with me," Nate said.

"I don't know how to play savor," Kerrigan said, feeling good again, with him, and about them.

"Each player, that would be you and me, must savor every moment. No looking too far ahead. We savor what is happening here and now and let the rest go. Those days, weeks, and months are not here yet. Why worry about anything other than right now? That is how you play savor."

"And what happens if I can't follow the game rules?" Kerrigan asked him as he inched closer to her.

"I'm a team player, so I will help you," he said, as she could feel his breath on hers. Their lips were inches apart.

"I don't even know how to start this game," Kerrigan said, teasing him, knowing he wanted to kiss her and she him.

"Oh that's easy," Nate replied. "The kick off begins by you holding my hand, like this," he said, touching her fingers and taking her hand into his own, "and then you walk with me into my bedroom and…"

"Nate, I can't stay the night," Kerrigan interrupted him and he put his finger to her lips.

"Whoa, savor, remember? You're thinking too far ahead. Morning is hours and hours away. Now is what we focus on, right now," he said pressing his lips to hers and she found herself responding to him with everything she had to give, once again.

"Now," she said, pulling away from their intense kissing, "Right now…" Then the two of them hurried down the hallway, into the bedroom and closed and locked the door behind them.

Chapter 10

Kerrigan returned to her beach house shortly after midnight and she fell into her bed feeling optimistic again. She expected to have ups and downs this summer, actually more downs, but the thoughts and feelings she already experienced had completely taken her by surprise. She knew her own heart and she was well aware of how hard she was falling for Nate Stein. She already loved him.

***

She could hardly wait to get back over to Nate and Meggie. Kerrigan was up early, showered and dressed, and was walking through the sand in front of Hallie's house when she noticed her window blinds open. Hallie was an early riser and Kerrigan smiled at the thought of her most likely watching out of one of her windows as Kerrigan made her way back to Nate and his little girl. This was a good thing for everyone, Kerrigan believed now more than ever.

As she stepped past Hallie's house, she heard a crash coming from inside of her house. Kerrigan immediately stopped walking to listen again. Nothing.

She turned around and quickly made her way up Hallie's deck and to the door. She knocked hard once and didn't wait as she opened the door and walked in. "Hallie? I heard a crash…" Not too far from the door, Kerrigan saw her dish from MJ's kitchen, the one she brought Hallie some soup in, shattered on the floor at her feet. The glass lid was also broken. And then she saw Hallie, down on the floor on her stomach, reaching for her, gasping for air.

"Oh my God! Hallie! Are you okay? Does anything hurt?" Hallie tried, but she could not speak. She could not get enough air into her lungs. Kerrigan knew right away it was not her heart. She went to her and helped her move flat on her back as she was still struggling for air. She kept holding her chest, which Kerrigan immediately noticed was moving in an abnormal way and she could hear whistling and wheezing sounds.

"Hallie, listen to me," Kerrigan instructed, "Try to take slow breaths, stay with me, I am going to call for an ambulance." Hallie nodded her head as Kerrigan ran into her kitchen to find the phone. She called 911 and she remained calm and informative while on the phone. She told them she suspected a collapsed lung, and to hurry because the patient, who has emphysema, was in a lot of pain. Hallie was not just any patient. Kerrigan had come to care deeply about her in such a short time. She needed her, and now she had to help her.

When the ambulance arrived, sirens blaring, Kerrigan was in full paramedic mode. She never stepped out of the way for them, she helped. They all agreed, while on the living room floor of Hallie's house, that she definitely had a collapsed lung. She was given oxygen as they loaded her up onto a stretcher and Nate appeared at the wide-open front door of Hallie's beach house, holding Meggie on his hip. "What happened?" he asked as Kerrigan looked up at him. She rushed over to him, and guided him and Meggie outside. She did not want Meggie to get scared, because right now she felt scared and she saw the same fear on Nate's face.

"Hallie is having trouble breathing and we need to take her to the hospital right now," Kerrigan said, reaching for Meggie's hand as Nate held her.

"Are you going with her in the ambulance?" he asked Kerrigan, and she replied *yes* as the Orange Beach paramedics began exiting the house with Hallie lying on the stretcher and Kerrigan followed them out.

Nate wanted to follow the ambulance to the hospital, but he didn't want to frighten Meggie any further. He decided to go back home and try to keep Meggie's mind occupied while he waited to hear any news from Kerrigan.

***

At the hospital, Kerrigan sat in the waiting room for an hour. She knew Hallie would be okay, she had to be okay, she needed her. Nate needed her, too. The worry in his eyes caught Kerrigan's attention earlier. He had only known Hallie for a matter of several months, and Kerrigan for just weeks. Still, they both cared about her…and loved her.

A short while later, Kerrigan had some answers. Hallie had a collapsed lung. The doctor reiterated everything that Kerrigan already was aware of. Patients who have emphysema are more likely to develop pneumothorax, which is a collapsed lung. Hallie's lungs are already so compromised, so this happening did not come as a surprise to the doctor. After Hallie's chest x-ray and CAT scan, the doctor told Kerrigan the only treatment needed was bed rest at home, and he ordered oxygen to be administered with a portable machine, as needed. He also told her that Hallie should not be alone.

When Kerrigan walked into the patient room where Hallie was temporarily resting, she found her hooked up to oxygen and coherent. "Well, look who's feeling better!" It was Kerrigan's turn to be there for this woman.

"Oh honey, you made such a fuss over me, calling an ambulance. I would have guessed it was just a goddamn gas bubble again," Hallie said, speaking slow and trying not to move the oxygen tubes inserted into her nostrils.

"It was a little more than you could just blow out your ass this time, Hallie," Kerrigan teased, and Hallie laughed too hard and began to cough.

"You're going to be fine," Kerrigan said to her after her cough settled. "Bed rest and some more of my homemade soup should take care of the problem."

"I broke your bowl," Hallie said, "I saw you walking by and I wanted to return your bowl and then I dropped the damn thing and fell down. Good thing I didn't cut myself in all that glass. I don't want any scars on my pretty face at my age."

Kerrigan giggled. "Oh no worries, Hallie. It's not my bowl, it's MJ's and I doubt she will miss it. Let's get you out of here so you can go home and clean up all that glass off of your living room floor." Hallie smiled at Kerrigan and reached for her hand, and Kerrigan took it into her own. "Thank you, honey, thank you."

***

Three hours later, Kerrigan was helping Hallie walk on the deck leading to her beach house, and when she opened the door Kerrigan reminded Hallie to watch out for the glass. She wanted to get Hallie seated in the recliner chair and then tend to the mess.

There was no mess left behind as Hallie and Kerrigan found Meggie kneeling by the coffee table in front of the couch, coloring, and Nate was walking out of the kitchen. Kerrigan had called him from the hospital to let him know about Hallie and when she told him she was coming back home today, he and Meggie took care of a few things inside of her house to welcome her back.

"You cleaned my floor, dear, and what are you cooking in my kitchen?" Hallie smiled underneath her oxygen-tube-filled nose as Kerrigan carried the portable tank and helped her sit down comfortably in the recliner, near Meggie.

"Dinner," Nate replied as Meggie blurted out, "What's that hanging out of your nose holes, Hallie?"

"I need a little help breathing, doll, that's all," Hallie replied. "I hope you know you have the best daddy in the world."

"I know, and now my mommy thinks so again, too," Meggie replied as everyone let that comment slide. She was just a little girl. Kids say things like that, but Kerrigan noticed how uncomfortable Nate looked.

There was no time to pull Nate aside, as the rest of the afternoon and early evening was spent taking care of Hallie. The four of them ate a seafood pasta bake that Nate prepared and even Meggie thought it was *yummy, especially the shrimp and the scallops under all that cheese.* After dinner, Hallie had tried to doze off in her recliner, but she wanted to pay attention to her company. Kerrigan realized Hallie needed some peace and quiet, so she suggested to Nate for he and Meggie leave.

"I was thinking the same thing," Nate responded. "Are you leaving, too?"

"No, the doctor does not want her to be alone, so I told Hallie I would stay with her."

"Kerrigan, we're right here, both of us on each side of her."

"I know, but I want to keep an eye on her for awhile, especially tonight. I can sleep on the couch here in case she needs anything."

"I'm right next door if you need help, okay?" Nate wanted to kiss her. They were standing in the kitchen and Hallie and Meggie were close by in the living room. "I'll miss you," he said, pulling her close and squeezing a cheek on her bottom with his entire hand.

"I'm just a house away," Kerrigan teased him, giving him a quick peck on the lips.

"Too far," he replied as they both walked into Hallie's living room. They had been worried something worse could have happened to Hallie today, and so relieved it had not. They now felt reassured and believed she was going to be fine… as were they.

Chapter 11

Seventy-two hours later, Hallie had to be checked out at the hospital again. It was a follow-up appointment for her to have another chest x-ray to see how well her lung was healing. The doctor informed her and Kerrigan that Hallie's lung was beginning to function properly again, but it may take a few weeks for her to have a full recovery. The doctor, while both Kerrigan and Hallie were in the exam room, reminded Hallie to follow his orders of slowly returning to her normal routine, and to stop sneaking cigarettes.

"Cigarettes?" Kerrigan asked, looking at the doctor and then at Hallie. "Have you seriously been smoking? When? I've been watching you for days!"

"If I cannot have one, just one, once in awhile, I may as well hang it up!" Hallie exclaimed and the doctor was not amused as he replied, "You are going to hang it up sooner than later if you don't listen to me."

When the doctor left the room, Kerrigan wanted to harp on this subject some more. "You still smoke? Didn't you learn what happened to your lungs from smoking in your younger days? I just assumed you gave it up!"

"At my age, if I want a goddamn cigarette, I will have one. I have enough sense to realize that smoking has done me no good and now it will just add to my misery, but I have my days, Kerrigan."

And that was all Hallie needed to say. Kerrigan refrained from questioning her or lecturing her anymore. She's eighty-three years old and has spent the past two decades dealing with a mother's unimaginable loss. *By all means, have a damn cigarette.*

***

Three days after her emergency, Hallie wanted to send Kerrigan home. They were sitting in her living room when she told her it was time.

"I really don't mind keeping an eye on you," Kerrigan replied.

"And I still expect you to," Hallie said, "just not around the clock. You need to resume your beach walks, your peace and quiet, and make the time to hook up with that cop next door." Kerrigan giggled, but she was not sure about leaving Hallie completely alone. She had gone home to shower and change clothes and she even left to get some groceries for Hallie's kitchen, but she had not been gone for long. She did miss getting exercise and just being outside, but Hallie had been too weak to move anywhere else beyond the couch to her bed to rest. And she most certainly missed Nate and Meggie.

"Go home and get something for me and come right back," Hallie told her.

"Okay, what do you want?" Kerrigan asked.

"That cell phone you claim to have shut off and put away," Hallie said. "If I am going to need to get ahold of you, you need to carry that damn phone. I know it puts you in touch with people back home, but that needs to come to a head to."

"What is this about, Hallie? I can put my number in your phone and I'll even keep my phone close-by at all times, but I'm nowhere near ready to take calls or reply to texts from a place that doesn't even seem like home to me anymore." Kerrigan felt defensive. She was not going to let Hallie, or anyone else, force her to do anything she was not ready for.

"I understand, just go get your damn phone so I can kick your ass out of my home," Hallie teased and Kerrigan shook her head at her when Hallie added, "I need my space… and a cigarette."

***

It wasn't nicotine, it was caffeine, and Kerrigan was enjoying a Diet Coke while sitting on her deck. She had her cell phone on the table near her, and it was on. There had been no more messages from Keith or Gail when she turned the phone back on and completely charged the battery again.

While lounging on her deck on one chair with her feet up on another, Kerrigan saw a woman getting out of a red Mustang convertible in the distance. She walked onto the beach, and when she got somewhat closer, Kerrigan recognized Bryn. She watched her walk straight up to Nate's house and let herself in. Kerrigan sat upright in her chair, planting her bare feet on the hot wooden deck as she made sure Nate's squad car was not parked up a ways next to her jeep or the little hottie's convertible. *They share a child, they will always be parents to Meggie, I'm sure she has a reason to stop by his house when he's not home.* Kerrigan still let it unnerve her. She found her flip flops on the deck under her chair and she slipped them on before walking the length of her deck. Back and forth. Repeating that process suddenly became pacing.

Just a few minutes later, Kerrigan saw Nate's front door open up and Bryn left again. She seemed to be on a mission, not having looked around at all. She just walked directly back to her car, got in, started it up, backed out, and drove away.

Kerrigan felt jealous. That woman rocked a pair of shorts and a tight top like Kerrigan never had. She would always have some sort of a hold on Nate because she's the mother of his child. Nate hadn't fallen out of love with her, he wanted her and their family. It was Bryn who wanted out, who divorced him. Maybe that meant Nate would always be vulnerable to her because a part of his heart remained fragile because of her. *Ridiculous! Nate cares about me. Nate wants me. I just need to feel more confident, more comfortable in my own skin.*

She walked over to Hallie's and checked on her. She found her sleeping comfortably in her recliner chair. Kerrigan tip toed back out of the house, picked up her cell phone on the table on her own deck and began walking the beach. She never took the time to go inside to find her tennis shoes. She just kicked off her flip flops on her deck and left them there. A barefoot walk in the sand felt nice.

When she was headed back toward her beach house, she was almost there when she saw him running toward her. He liked to go for a run after work, before he cooked dinner for himself, and before Hallie's incident he had been cooking for them. Kerrigan missed him, but she didn't want to appear needy. She felt like her walls were up again, especially since she saw his ex-wife coming and going from his home.

"Hi there," Nate said, coming to a stop in front of her. She noticed he had not broken a sweat yet as she looked up at him. "I hope this means Hallie is feeling well enough to give you a much-needed break."

"She is doing better, but I'm on call if she needs me," Kerrigan said, holding up her phone.

"What if I need you?" he asked, putting his hands on her upper arms, right above her elbows.

"You have my number," Kerrigan responded as Nate gently rubbed her arms, up and down.

"911? Because it is an emergency." Nate laughed at his own comment and Kerrigan joined him. "Oh I'm sure it only feels urgent," she said.

"Oh it definitely feels urgent," he said, laughing and then she broke the mood.

"Something else must have been urgent today as I saw your ex-wife pop in and out of your home." Kerrigan told him as she watched his face for any signs. Signs that he might still care for her. Signs that he was hiding something.

"She does that sometimes," Nate said. "Today, she needed to pick up my insurance card. She lost her copy and needed mine because Meggie is on my insurance and she had to take her to the dentist."

"Oh, I hope Meggie is okay," Kerrigan said, feeling foolish for being jealous.

"Other than eating too damn much candy, she is fine. She has a cavity already at four years old. Bryn knows I'm pissed." Nate said, shaking his head.

"That's not good," Kerrigan replied.

"So did it bother you to see Bryn today?" Nate asked her, putting her right, square on that awkward spot.

"Bother is such a strong word…" Kerrigan replied.

Nate laughed at her. "You're kinda sexy when you're jealous."

"Call me later," Kerrigan said, as she walked off.

"What?" Nate called after her.

"Get your run in, but don't wear yourself out…I'm going to need you energetic later." Kerrigan yelled out to him as she continued to walk away and Nate let out a very loud, *woohoo,* as he began to run on the beach in the opposite direction.

***

Awhile later, Kerrigan decided to walk over to Nate's house. When she opened his front door, she was not expecting what she saw. Meggie was running around in the living room and Bryn was sitting on the couch. It was not yet the weekend and from the conversation she shared earlier on the beach with Nate, she knew he was not expecting her tonight.

Kerrigan didn't knock before walking in, and now she wished she had. "Oh, hi," Kerrigan muttered as Bryn looked up from where she was sitting on the middle of the couch with her legs crisscrossed. She could have been doing yoga for all Kerrigan knew, but her mere presence there, tonight, bothered Kerrigan.

"Meggie missed her daddy," Bryn said to Kerrigan as if to clarify why she was there, and by now Meggie had run to Kerrigan and she immediately picked her up. Those soft red curls and freckled face melted Kerrigan's heart.

"My mommy misses my daddy sometimes," the four-year-old spoke outright and Kerrigan kept herself from glancing over at Bryn, still on the couch. "Where is your daddy?" Kerrigan asked as Nate came walking down the hallway and into the living room.

"Hi," Kerrigan said to him, as he smiled at her and said, "Hi yourself." He wanted to tell her that dinner would be on hold for awhile, until he managed to spend a little time his daughter and then pacify her mother.

"Should I come back later?" Kerrigan spoke, softly to him with her back turned to Bryn.

"Give me a half an hour and I will be over. We can order out for dinner, your choice," Nate told her as she hugged Meggie goodbye and waved her hand in the air at Bryn who looked a little too comfortable on Nate's couch and in his home. Kerrigan couldn't help but see the irony in this situation. Just a little over a week ago, she was sitting in that exact spot on Nate's couch and Bryn obviously had a problem with that.

Exactly thirty-five minutes passed before Nate came walking through her door. Kerrigan had been acting busy in the kitchen, trying not to let her mind go there. Bryn was up to something.

"It's so good to finally be alone with you," Nate said, walking through her house and toward her. He never said another word as he took her into his arms and kissed her hard and full on the mouth. Kerrigan responded and then she pulled away from him.

"Talk to me. She wants something, what is it?"

"She and Jenny are having some problems."

"So she comes running to you for comfort?"

"That is pretty much what I told her, too."

"And her response was?"

"She wants me back..."

Kerrigan felt her heart sink. She knew. She knew it by the way Bryn reacted to her being near Nate and Meggie. She caught every one of those daggers she had been shooting at her, glance after glance. *But how in the hell can a woman be gay one minute and now not be?* "She wants you back as in back in her bed? Won't it be a little crowded in there with another woman on her mind?" Kerrigan felt angry and Nate understood.

"You're not thinking anything different than I am," Nate said to her, still standing in the same spot on the living room floor where he had just taken her into his arms moments ago. "She's such a mess. Jenny will be back and the two of them will kiss and make up, or whatever it is they do."

"Is that how you really feel?" Kerrigan asked him.

"Kerrigan, she is my ex-wife. She can't just change her mind like the wind changes directions. She put me through hell when she tore apart our family."

"Your family, Nate. Meggie. You need to think about her." Kerrigan heard those words escape her mouth, but she didn't want to say them. She loved Meggie and she wanted that little girl to be happy, but she thought she was happy with her mom's life and her dad's life, which now was beginning to include Kerrigan.

"I am thinking about her," Nate responded. "She has adjusted so well to our craziness. Mom lives one place with her girlfriend, and dad lives alone on the beach. She does fine with having two homes. What would happen if we jumbled all that up again for her?"

"I think the question is, do you want to jumble all that up for the sake of having your family back?" Kerrigan's voice sounded strong, but inside she was coming undone. Just the thought of losing him, them, hurt. And that's what she was afraid of from the very beginning of this. She wanted to avoid the pain. *And, dammit, here it is.*

"No," was all Nate said.

"Are you sure?" Kerrigan asked him.

"I've never been more sure," he said, taking her into his arms and pulling her close. He held her for a moment, and after she reached her arms around him and tightened them, she slowly began to unleash her hold.

"I want you to go," Kerrigan told him as she pulled completely out of his arms. "I want you to think about this, sleep on it, pray about it. I cannot continue down this road with you until I know for sure Bryn won't turn your head again."

"No, that's absurd. I already told her, I'm with you." Nate felt panicked as he defended himself, and them. Someone had to. She appeared to be giving up way too quickly. Too damn easily.

"A part of me is with you, too." Kerrigan said. "And another part of me has a lot of baggage back in Baltimore. Not in my heart, but on paper I am still married. I think this is a warning sign, a siren blaring in our faces right now. We both need to be sure, we both need to offer one-hundred percent of ourselves to each other – or this will not work."

Nate shook his head no. "You're wrong! It is working. Don't mess it all up now. I need you, I need this feeling you bring to my life – and I know you feel it too and you need me every ounce as much."

"I do," Kerrigan said, feeling her bottom lip quiver and her voice crack. "That is why I want you to come back. Come back to me when I'm divorced, and when you're sure." Kerrigan turned away from him. She intended to – and she tried to – walk into the kitchen and wait there until he left.

"I told her I love you."

Kerrigan stopped walking, and she slowly turned her body back around to face him. "Say it again…"

"I…love…you." he said, slowly, taking steps toward her.

"Savor that feeling," Kerrigan told him.

Chapter 12

It wasn't supposed to hurt like this. Kerrigan wanted to avoid the hurt. That is why she did it. That is why she told Nate their relationship had to wait. But, as soon as Nate walked away, Kerrigan was overwhelmed with sadness and she feared she had really lost him, for good.

Hallie was awake in her recliner when Kerrigan walked in.

"My God, honey," Hallie said after taking one look at Kerrigan. "Sit down, let's talk it out." Kerrigan immediately burst into tears and Hallie got up out of her chair to sit beside her on the couch and hold her. This young woman had already become like a daughter to Hallie, and right now she just wanted to take away her pain. "I know it hurts, I know we have shitty days when we dwell and need to cry. I'm here for you, honey."

"I need reassurance that I did the right thing…" Kerrigan said, through her tears. And then she told Hallie the entire story. Hallie was silent for a few minutes before she spoke.

"I know how much Nate loved his wife and the idea of having a family and living happily ever after," she began, "but I also know he has been slapped in the face with the reality of how you can plan your life one way and just like that it can all be blown to bits. I think a few months ago, Nate may have jumped at the chance to take her back. I think he had hoped she would change her mind and come back. But, a lot has happened since then. He has watched her replace him with another woman, their divorce is final, their little girl has adjusted so well to their new and separate lives… and he met you."

Kerrigan shook her head through her tears. "That's pretty much the same as he said to me, but I can't give him what he wants. Not yet. I have unresolved matters in my life…and I think he might, too."

"He will wait for you," Hallie said, patting and then squeezing Kerrigan's hands which were resting on her lap.

"So what do I do?" Kerrigan asked, feeling like she had never needed guidance more than she did right now. She was grieving from losing her baby, she was still married, and she had unresolved issues with Gail. And now there's Nate. And Meggie. *Her future? Not if she didn't grab ahold of it while it's within her grasp.*

***

She didn't want to do it. She debated. She waited. She stalled. Her phone was right in front of her because she had an agreement with Hallie to keep it close-by in case she needed her. She picked up her phone off of the end of the bed, found Keith's name in her contact list, and she called him.

He answered on the third ring. "Kerrie?" She paused, or more like froze. *Could she really do this?* She knew she didn't have to face him or anything until the end of summer, if ever, if she didn't want to. She had been gone for a month, and now she had to say something to him.

"Yes, it's me," she said into the phone as she paced the floor in the bedroom of the beach house.

"It's good to hear your voice," Keith said. "How are you? He wanted to add *and where are you,* but he was afraid too many questions too fast would overwhelm her. She had ignored all of his previous attempts to call or text her.

"I'm okay," she replied. "How are you?"

"Pretty good. I'm glad you called. I've been worried about you," Keith admitted.

"No need to be, I'm fine." Kerrigan said wondering what he expected from her at this point.

"You don't have to tell me, but I would like to know where you are," Keith said, feeling a little bolder.

"Orange Beach, at MJ's place," she confessed.

"That's a long drive, Kerrie. Did the jeep hold up okay?" Keith always kept her old jeep in running condition. He was her personal mechanic. She appreciated the times throughout their relationship and five-year marriage when he would change her oil, rotate her tires, and just keep the jeep in running condition. Most recently, he had told her the jeep's tires were thinning and needed to be replaced.

"Yes, it's my old faithful, you know it has never let me down." Kerrigan started to smile.

"Which is more than you can say for me..." Keith replied.

"Life let us both down," Kerrigan said, feeling like she no longer wanted to blame him.

"So where do we go from here, Kerrie?" Keith asked her. "Do you want to come home?"

"Yes, I do." There was silence on his end of the phone before she continued speaking. "I have to get the rest of my things...we have to decide what to do about our stuff and the house... and one of us needs to file for a divorce." It was a lot to say in one response, but they both needed closure.

"I have an attorney, Kerrigan." *Of course he did. Gail most likely hired one for him.*

"Are you still living in the house?" Kerrigan could no longer bring herself to say *our house*.

"I put it up for sale." He never answered her question so Kerrigan assumed his answer was he had already moved in with Gail, into her house.

"I would like to come and get what's mine." She couldn't bring herself to say it, she could not ask if he had already been through the nursery, Piper's things. If he allowed Gail to do it, Kerrigan was going to blow a gasket.

"I want you to do that, and Kerrigan...?" Keith's voice changed to almost a whisper. "Will you help me pack up her room?" She closed her eyes on the other end of the phone, hoping perhaps that gesture would somehow help to keep the tears in.

"I will," she answered, trying to sound strong, trying not to bawl her eyes out right at this moment. "I will be home by the end of the week, but just so you know it's only a trip to do what we have to do... to move on... because I'm not staying... I'm not going to live in Baltimore, ever again."

"Where will you live?" he asked her, finding it impossible to believe their marriage was over and he would probably never see her again once they divided their things into his and hers and closed the door on their life together by severing their marriage. With the assistance of a wealthy attorney friend of Gail's, she ensured Keith's divorce from Kerrigan wouldn't be drawn out – because she wanted it to happen overnight.

"I'm going to stay here in Orange Beach until I figure that out," Kerrigan answered him. "I have MJ's house until the end of summer while she's backpacking around Europe."

Keith let out a small chuckle on his end of the phone. "Leave it to MJ. We should all be so lucky to live so carefree."

"I owe her…I needed this escape," Kerrigan admitted.

"Are you lonely there?" he asked her.

Lonely? Kerrigan thought about her first day at the beach house and how Hallie became a pain in her ass very quickly. Then she thought of meeting her *other* neighbor and his sweet little girl. Meeting Nate had already changed her. She was not going to allow herself to feel guilty for falling in love with another man and even wishing for a whole new life, because she could pretty much guarantee Keith had not been faithfully waiting around for her return. "No, Keith. I'm not lonely."

"Good," he said, and she could hear him breathing hard into the phone.

"I'll be home, I mean, I'll be back in a few days." Kerrigan said not knowing what else they would talk about during this phone conversation and she suddenly wanted to cut it short.

"I'm not crazy about you driving," Keith said. "Why don't you book a flight?"

"I can't…my stuff, remember? I need to pack the jeep."

"Never mind," Keith replied. "Just be careful, and let me know…"

"Okay, bye." Kerrigan was ready to end their call when she heard him say, "Thanks for calling." She replied, "you're welcome," and disconnected the call.

***

Kerrigan spent the next two days making sure Hallie was well enough to be left alone. She felt guilty for leaving, but she explained to Hallie what she was going to do and how badly she wanted to return to Orange Beach afterward. Hallie reassured Kerrigan she would be fine alone, and reminded her that Nate was also nearby if she needs anything. Kerrigan never told Nate she was leaving. She had not seen him again since he left her house that night, after he told her he loved her.

At daybreak, Kerrigan packed a small overnight bag that she had found in MJ's closet. She wouldn't need much to stay in Baltimore for a day or two. It was not going to be an easy trip, but she felt like she was in a better place now, mentally. She would find closure and then return to the beach. She owed it to herself to help Keith pack up the house, and finalize their divorce.

As Kerrigan walked in the sand and up to her jeep parked on the road above the beach houses, she noticed her jeep was not in the parking spot she had left it. Or maybe she was wrong, maybe she had parked it on the end the last time she drove it. No, she felt certain it had definitely been moved and what Kerrigan spotted next amazed her. She knew every inch of that jeep. She had been driving it for ten years. She realized instantly, as she looked down at it and then walked around to the other side to do the same, her jeep had four brand new tires.

She looked downhill at the beach houses and saw him. Nate was standing there, on his deck, watching her. He knew that she knew. She made eye contact with him. "You did this, didn't you?" she hollered over to him as he hopped the railing and landed on both of his bare feet in the sand. As he walked toward her, she felt like running to him to meet him halfway. She wanted this man to hold her and never let her go. But, she could not do that. Not yet. Not until she made this trip. The trip for which she now did not have to worry about getting a flat tire and not knowing how to change it.

When he reached her, she smiled at him. "I don't have the money right now to repay you, but I will. Thank you, Nate, I mean it. You have no idea how–"

"How bald your tires were?" he interrupted. "A friend of mine is a mechanic. He owed me one. You were in desperate need of new tires and what kind of man would I be if I let you travel unsafely too damn far by yourself?"

She smiled at him. "I think I know what kind of man you are, Nate Stein."

"Then take me with you."

"What?" she asked.

"I will stay out of the way, just take me along for the ride. I can pack clean underwear in a matter of minutes." He knew the chances of Kerrigan agreeing were slim, but he had nothing to lose by asking because he was scared of losing her. He wanted her to come back to Orange Beach. Hallie told him about her plans, and he wanted to believe it would be that easy for Kerrigan to wrap up her old life and leave it behind.

"Nate, I need to do this alone, but I love you for offering." Yes, she said it. She said those three little words without even thinking. Her heart spoke. Her heart didn't care about thinking first. It only cared about feeling. Her eyes widened and she looked down at her feet. By now, Nate was standing closer to her.

"I heard that." He was smiling and almost felt giddy with her. *She loved him, too!*

"I, I don't know what to say."

"Did it slip out?" Nate teased her.

"Yeah," she giggled and that feeling was back. Life was so easy with him. They have fun. They laugh. And they love.

Lori Bell

"Just savor it," Nate said as he leaned toward her, lifted her chin with two fingers and kissed her goodbye.

Chapter 13

Kerrigan, once again, drove seventeen consecutive hours with only a few stops to fill up her gas tank, empty her bladder, and get another Diet Coke. This time her commute brought her back to Baltimore, Maryland to the home she left, and already, it did not feel like home to her anymore.

She texted Keith after she was on the road for twelve hours and she told him she would see him in five. He didn't like the idea of her driving that far, that long, alone. But, to him, she didn't feel much like his wife anymore and wouldn't be for much longer, so he kept those worries to himself and just told her to *be safe*.

The sound of her jeep on the rock driveway forced Kerrigan back to the reality of why she was here, why she came back. She put her phone and her keys in her handbag and got out of the jeep with it. She left her overnight bag and her open can of Diet Coke in the vehicle as she slowly walked up to the house. It was dark, nearly midnight, and Keith had the porch light on. For her, she assumed. And, God, she prayed he was in there alone. She didn't need an in-her-face reminder of Gail's betrayal.

The door was unlocked and Kerrigan let herself in. The living room was dim-lit and she saw him lying on the couch, sleeping. She walked over to him, thinking how many times he had fallen asleep watching television before bedtime and she would nudge him or kiss him awake and tell him it was time to go to bed. She didn't want him to wake with a start to find her staring at him, so she touched his arm and softly said his name. He opened his eyes instantly and sat upright.

"Hi, wow, it's late. I'm glad you made it," Keith said stretching his shoulders and back a little.

"It is late, I'm sorry I couldn't get here earlier. I left at daybreak."

"You must be exhausted," he stated.

"A little," she replied.

"Are you hungry?" Keith always had something to eat in the refrigerator, and Kerrigan actually had been living totally the opposite in Orange Beach. She ate well at Hallie's and with Nate, but she had not done much cooking for just herself.

"Maybe a little. What did you have for dinner tonight?" Kerrigan asked.

"I grilled steaks, and I have a baked potato and some greens left with it. If you want, I can heat a plate for you." Kerrigan did want to eat and she told him as much as he got up off of the couch and went into the kitchen while she followed him.

"I thought you weren't living here," she said as he opened the refrigerator and she noticed it was not as fully stocked as it used to be.

"I'm not, but I came here after work tonight with a few groceries and I grilled because I knew you would be sucking Diet Coke the whole way here and needing some food in your stomach." Kerrigan was touched.

"You didn't have to go through any trouble, but thank you," she said, sitting down at the table. It didn't feel like their kitchen anymore. She felt like a guest in an unfamiliar home.

"You're welcome. Eat."

***

After she ate, Kerrigan walked back into the living room and took the throw off of the back of the couch and covered herself up with it as she sat there. She had worn just another oversized t-shirt and athletic shorts with flip flops for the drive, and now she had her shoes off and her bare feet curled up under her on the couch. Keith smiled when he walked back into the room and saw her.

"Cold? Or just wanting to get comfy?" he asked.

"I am comfy," she smiled.

"Good," he said, sitting down beside her, but not too close.

"So what's the plan?" she asked him, wondering if he was going to stay there tonight or go back to Gail's house.

"I guess we will get a few hours of sleep tonight and then pack up tomorrow." He never said where he was sleeping.

"Are you coming back in the morning?"

"No. I'm staying here tonight. I will take the couch, you can have our bed, um, the bed." It was not awkward between them, but it certainly was not the same.

"You don't have to do that." Kerrigan actually wanted to be there in the house, by herself, for one more night.

"Kerrie, this was our home, we owe it to each other to find some sort of closure, together."

"You're right," she said, wondering if he received the divorce papers yet.

"So, has your time in Orange Beach been good for you?" Keith could tell something has changed. She looked better, he noticed her tan skin. He hasn't seen her with such great color, ever. They always worked too much and never took any vacations, not even a honeymoon. They bought their house right before they got married and then they both agreed to save some money. She also seemed more in control of her emotions, not depressed or distraught anymore.

"It has. I love the beach and the sun, and my neighbors are wonderful. I showed up wanting to be alone out there, but that hasn't been the case. I've learned how we are here for the sake of each other in this life. I don't want to be alone, and I don't want you to be either, Keith." They had not talked about Gail yet.

"I wanted to be here for you, after…" He didn't want to say it, and he also didn't want to talk about Gail.

"I know, but I couldn't let you or anyone else in…and when I saw you with Gail, I knew we were lost and had been for a very long time," Kerrigan admitted to him.

"One kiss did not mean our marriage had to be over," Keith said, trying to downplay it.

"No, but it's more than that. We both know it. We all three know it. I just hope she's good to you. You deserve that." Kerrigan didn't know if this would have been half as easy to let go of him had she not met Nate and felt, really felt, what a relationship should be like. She and Keith lacked so much, that was evident to her now, and she wanted to know if what he'd tucked away in his heart for many years had been unlocked and revived. She needed to know.

"She's not going to chew me up and spit me out, Kerrie."

"No? Well, that's good." Kerrigan smiled.

"I want you to be happy, too." Keith wondered if she ever would open herself up to loving a man again. It pained him to think this, but he hoped she would find love and be able to become pregnant again. She would have been an amazing mother to Piper, had she been given a lifetime with her.

"I will be. I just need to get through the next couple of days." She felt that familiar sick feeling in the pit of her stomach. She had to pack up everything she owned, she had to go into the nursery again, and she expected to talk to an attorney about the disband of their marriage.

"I will get you through it," he said. "Just let me be here for you, one last time." Kerrigan took his hand in hers and held it.

***

After very little sleep, Kerrigan woke up on the couch to find Keith asleep in the living room chair with his feet up on the ottoman. She remembered him telling her that he didn't want to sleep in the bed either. It just didn't feel right to either of them anymore.

Kerrigan took a shower, put on some clean clothes that she found in her closet in their old bedroom. She was tickled to find a pair of size fourteen black Bermuda shorts had fit. She was a size sixteen before her pregnancy. Her walks, and running spurts, on the beach were beginning to pay off a little. She did feel less jiggly in places. She put on a t-shirt with those shorts. After she blow-dried her hair in the bathroom, she came out to find Keith cooking breakfast. He had bacon and eggs with buttered English muffins hot and ready for her.

"All you've done since I got here is feed me. Don't you think we should get some packing done?" Kerrigan asked him as she sat down and immediately took a strip of bacon and bit it.

"Not on an empty stomach," Keith replied.

Once they ate, he told Kerrigan to start looking through the kitchen cabinets and drawers and to take whatever she wanted. He reminded her of the toaster and coffee maker on the counter top, too.

"Coffee is your thing, Keith, but I will take the toaster if you don't want it." She also packed up a few dishes that had been her favorites and then she told him he could have or get rid of the rest.

Next, they moved into the living room. "Wanna sell

the furniture with the house?" she asked him, knowing she could not transport it in her jeep and he did not need it, living at Gail's. It wouldn't be good enough for her anyway.

"If you want to," he said.

"I want this blanket," she said taking it off the couch from where she left it when she woke up this morning, and she folded it into fours and tucked it under her arm as Keith laughed at her.

In their bedroom, all of Keith's clothes and things were already gone. Kerrigan took the rest of her clothes out of the closets and drawers and piled all of it up on the bed as Keith brought her some boxes to pack it all in. There wasn't anything left in the bathroom that she wanted to take with her, so she and Keith closed and taped the packed boxes and carried all of them out to her jeep. On their first trip outside, Keith was observant, as Kerrigan expected. "Did you get new tires?" he asked her and she wasn't quite sure how she was going to answer that question without bringing up Nate. She did not want to tell him about Nate. She, herself, could not believe he had come into her life and already changed it.

"Uh, yes, I did. My neighbor actually got them for me." Kerrigan tried to explain, while still being vague.

"Your neighbor, huh? Wow, MJ is one lucky girl to have such generous neighbors." Keith said, feeling grateful knowing Kerrigan was safer on the road than he originally thought. He never asked another question about the neighbor. Kerrigan knew the thought of her already being in

Heartless

a relationship would never cross Keith's mind.

Once the jeep was loaded down, they went back inside the house. Neither of them wanted to do what came next. They both stood in the living room. Keith had his hands in the front pockets of his jeans as he rocked back and forth on the heels of his well-worn tennis shoes and Kerrigan stood behind the couch near him. "I don't want to do this," she said feeling the tears well up in her eyes. He reached for her hand and held it.

Chapter 14

Kerrigan went first. She stood in front of the closed nursery door for a moment before she reached for the door handle, turned it, and slowly pushed the door open. Keith turned on the light and the ceiling fan began to turn, too. Kerrigan saw the crib, the changing table, the stroller tucked away in a corner. The stroller she never took a ride in, never had a chance to, because her life ended after only five weeks. Five weeks of amazing. Those beginning weeks with a new baby are new and exciting and can be stressful, exhausting, and worrisome too. But, not for Kerrigan. She had waited too long to hold a baby of her own in her arms. Every second counted, every minute was precious to her. And she was so grateful for that now.

Kerrigan walked over to the rocking chair and remembered the last time she sat in it, holding her lifeless baby, begging God to give her back, and swearing she would never let her go. The tears were spilling over in her eyes as she sat down again in that same rocker, bent forward, and put her face in her hands. Keith didn't hesitate, he was on his knees in front of her, wrapping his arms around her, putting his face close to hers. "This is so fucking unfair," he said to his wife, through his own tears. They both cried and held each other, which was something they should have done months ago.

"I want this rocker," Kerrigan said, trying to find her composure again.

"Of course, Kerrie. I want you to have all of this, the crib too. You will be glad, one day, that you kept it."

"I don't have room in my jeep for all of it."

"I will have it sent to you. Don't worry about that. Just keep it, store it somewhere for as long as you need to. It's yours." It was settled. All of the nursery furniture and baby gear would be packed up and sent to Orange Beach. Keith began taking apart the crib, and Kerrigan knew she had to go through the closet. There were two empty boxes in the hallway to use. She walked over to the closet door and opened it. She felt beaten. She felt on the brink, again. But somehow the thought of getting this done, getting out of there, leaving Baltimore and starting a new life in Orange Beach, empowered her to finish this. She was tired of the pain, tired of feeling sadness. Now, she only sought closure.

Two boxes were full of baby clothes as Keith finished taking apart the crib. He folded the crib sheet, mattress pad, and bumper pad and put it inside one of the clothes boxes that Kerrigan had filled. She resisted the urge to take the small fitted sheet, unfold it, and bring it to her face. She wanted to smell it, just as she had Piper's yellow baby blanket. When she looked back into the closet, she saw the onesie which had fallen on the floor, and when she bent down to pick it up, her eyes widened. Keith watched her remove the tiny pink onesie from a hanger and then she handed it to him. "I want you to have this," her voice cracked. He took the onesie from her and turned it around to read the embroidery on the front. *Daddy's little girl.*

Keith felt his insides crumbling. It was the familiar helpless feeling he had that day when he bolted into the nursery to find his wife on the floor, trying to revive their baby. He stood there with the onesie in both of his open hands and then he completely covered his face with it and broke down.

Kerrigan went to him and wrapped her arms around him. "I am so sorry," she said. "You were robbed of her, too," she cried, "and I was so consumed with grief and so heartless toward you." Keith pulled her closer and held her as both of their faces were wet with tears. They lost their baby, they lost their marriage, but somehow they had found a way to give each other closure today.

***

It was beginning to get dark when Kerrigan and Keith finished packing everything. Kerrigan looked at the round, Roman numeral clock on the living room wall when they came into the house after bringing the last of the boxes to her jeep. "I wasn't planning to stay another night," she said, wondering if she had the energy to get on the road and drive straight through back to Orange Beach. She didn't have the extra money to waste on staying overnight at a hotel. She told Keith while they were eating breakfast this morning that she called their boss and resigned from her job as a paramedic. Keith asked her if she wanted to work as an EMT in Orange Beach, and she told him she was done. Any job will have to do for awhile, she said, and Kerrigan decided to start applying when she returned to the beach house. Keith told her to use their credit card until she got on her feet, if she needed to. But, Kerrigan didn't want to put him further in debt. They didn't have much savings together, and now separately it was worse.

"You are not driving back all night long. We have a few more things to settle," Keith said, standing on his tip-toes and reaching for the clock on the wall that Kerrigan had just looked at. "This has to come down," he said, "and I've decided the furniture in here is going into storage for you, too. I know you're not settled and you won't be until you leave MJ's place, so I want you to let me know when you're ready for furniture and I will send a U-haul to you."

Kerrigan was taken aback. "Keith, I can't."

"Yes, you can. You will need it, I don't. Just let me do this for you. Consider it a divorce present." Keith smiled and

Kerrigan laughed at him. "I don't think there is such a thing...and we are not normal," she said.

Kerrigan thanked Keith again for being so generous with their things. He told her he wanted to do it, and he reminded her how he will take care of trying to sell the house. They were eating a pizza at the kitchen table, which was another piece of furniture going to be sent to storage for Kerrigan, when Keith got up and opened a cabinet drawer. He pulled out a pile of papers and set them down beside her plate. *Divorce papers.*

She stared for a few seconds at those papers, and then at Keith. She should have known. John Thomas Law Firm. Gail had lots of friends in high places. She used her connection to a wealthy attorney to rush this. She wanted Keith divorced quickly, and he was about to be. "Sad, but not as sad as it could be. Does that make sense?" she asked him. "I mean, I know we can't be happy together anymore, so let's hold on to how we still care about each other and wish each other the kind of happiness we failed to find together."

"You are something else, Kerrie," Keith said, reaching for her hand on the table, near their divorce papers. "That is exactly what I want for you. Be happy, and love someone like only you can love, with everything you've got."

"I do like to throw it all out there, don't I?" Kerrigan laughed. "It can be overwhelming, I've been told...by Gail." And there it was. The subject the two of them needed to address. Keith just looked at her. He didn't want to go there.

"I am going to sign this right now," Kerrigan said as she scribbled her first and last name quickly on the line on the page in front of her, "and then we are going to talk about my best friend."

She tried not to think about the finality of it. Her signature underneath his. Their marriage was officially over. They were divorced. She stood up and walked over to set the papers on the kitchen counter and then she turned back around to find Keith pushing the paper plate, with a half eaten slice of pizza on it, away from his reach.

"Do you feel like she's your soul mate? Do you feel like the rest of the world does not exist when she's in your arms?" Kerrigan was making Keith feel awkward.

"Why are you asking me this? We don't need to talk about my relationship with Gail. It will only hurt you, Kerrie." Keith remained seated at the kitchen table.

"It will hurt me if it doesn't work out with you and her." Kerrigan was being honest.

"What?" Keith asked her.

"Yeah, sounds strange, I know, but I don't want to find out that she's hurt you. I know how much you want to be with her. You love her, you always have." Kerrigan walked over to him and stood directly in front of his legs.

"I loved you, too." he said, looking up at her.

"We make better buddies than we do lovers." Kerrigan winked at him.

"I'm going to be sad to see you leave here again, because I know you…and you won't be back." Keith looked at her and she knew he had read her mind.

"No, I won't. There is too much pain here. It's just easier not to be close to where we lost her. I just want to get to that point, wherever I am, to learn to live with it. I want to heal." Kerrigan knew she was on the right path to getting there. Hallie was her godsend, she taught her how to grieve and still live. And Nate taught her how to love again. She missed them both already.

"Just let me know how you are once in awhile," Keith said, taking both of her hands into his as he stood up to meet her height. He also was five-foot, eight. "I mean it. Don't make me worry about you." He opened his arms and Kerrigan curled herself into his chest.

***

The sun was beginning to rise. The papers were signed and left inside of the house. Her jeep was completely jam-packed with boxes, she couldn't even see out of her rearview mirror. Kerrigan had already said goodbye to Keith in the house, and she asked him not to walk her outside. It was going to be difficult enough for her to leave.

She had tears, she felt the loss of her marriage and her baby surface in her heart as she backed her jeep out of the rock drive-way one last time. She turned the radio up in hopes of shifting her mind's focus away from how sad this was. She drove through town and as she steered her jeep around the bend, she was almost there. Keith had told her the headstone was now in place. At first, Kerrigan said she didn't want to see it. It would just be too hard. She was still trying to talk herself out of going there as she reached the cemetery on the outskirts of the city. With mixed emotions, she turned onto the premises.

She sat in her jeep for a few minutes. *It's still not too late to leave. Don't do this to yourself.* Kerrigan got out, and walked slowly through the tall, green grass. The tombstone was small, just as Piper had been. The words engraved into the stone were painful to read… *Piper Rose Ross…Eternally in our hearts.*

Kerrigan was numb as she stood there, looking at something so final before her eyes. She wouldn't let the pain come rushing back. She couldn't. It was crippling enough at times and this was not going to be one of those times for her. The longer she stood there, suddenly the angrier she became.

Keith was right, she thought of him and what he had said to her in the nursery. "How fucking unfair!" she screamed out loud as she looked up at the white puffy clouds in the blue sky above her. "She was mine! I tried so hard and I waited so long for her! I had so many plans! What did I ever do to deserve this? You never gave me a chance! How am I supposed to trust that you won't send me more pain and suffering? Before you do that…God…look at me…I can't handle anymore!" The tears were there now. It was like a dam had been broken in her heart. She was flooded with emotion, so much pain, again. Her baby was in the ground underneath her. She had been shown no mercy.

Kerrigan no longer felt strong as she made her way down into the grass, crisscrossed her legs, and put her face in her hands. She cried until she had no more tears left, and then she got up, kissed two fingers on her hand and touched the top of her baby girl's headstone. "I love you so much, Piper." She couldn't do this to herself. She couldn't come back here ever again. "I know you are not really here. You're with me. You're in my heart. Always."

She didn't turn back again, as she put one foot in front of the other in the tall, green grass and slowly walked back to her jeep. When she reached the driver's side of her jeep she was startled to see another vehicle parked behind hers. She had not seen or heard anyone pull up while she was at Piper's gravesite. She would know that sport utility vehicle anywhere. A shiny, black Suburban with Gail behind the wheel.

Chapter 15

They made eye contact as Gail remained inside of her vehicle. Kerrigan felt ice cold looking at her. Her best friend. The sister she believed was hers for life. Gone. And why? Because that is what Gail Boyd does. She loves and she leaves.

Kerrigan was not going to do this. She and Keith worked through all of the pain and hard feelings the past two days. They ended their marriage on a good note. Neither of them knew if their relationship would continue as friends, but they both had hoped for it to. Gail was an altogether different story. She was the reason Kerrigan walked away. When Keith turned to her, she didn't flinch, she didn't balk, she just opened her arms – *and no doubt her legs too* – and stole him away from Kerrigan.

Despite the fact that Kerrigan knew she and Keith were not meant to be, it still burned how Gail stepped in and picked up where she left off. And it would always burn. Kerrigan watched as Gail opened her car door and a black stiletto reached the rock-covered ground. *What could she possibly have to say for herself now?*

Kerrigan did not want to know. She opened her jeep door, got in, closed the door quickly, and turned the key in the ignition. What seemed like a second later, Gail was standing in front of her closed jeep door and staring at her through the window.

"Don't leave." Kerrigan watched her say those words through the glass. She read her lips because she couldn't hear her over the noise of the jeep's engine. A part of her wanted to throw the gear into drive and peel out of there. She was looking at a woman she loved pretty much her whole life. She was family to her. There she stood with her long blonde hair in an updo, wearing a black skirt short enough to risk sitting down in, and a form-fitting, red top. She dressed to the nines to run a gym and Kerrigan was more annoyed by her now than ever, wondering if she would cheat on Keith and break his heart again.

Kerrigan shut off the engine and got out. She didn't want to waste the gas on her, and it was hot inside the jeep. When Kerrigan stepped out, she felt the way she had felt many times being with Gail. Not good enough. Kerrigan had worn those comfortable athletic shorts, an oversized t-shirt and flip flops for the incredibly long drive ahead of her. She felt fat and unattractive standing next to Gail who was dressed up with perfectly applied makeup next to Kerrigan's none. She used to not let it bother her. She was not a fancy person. She was more simple. She didn't care about the name brands and the form-fitting clothes. She didn't have a shapely figure to fit into any clothes worth spending money on – money that she didn't have. And, Gail, had it all. Money. The fabulously fit body. Men. And now Keith.

"I wondered how this would feel," Kerrigan said standing before Gail, holding her own even though she felt like she was coming undone.

"How does it feel, Kerrigan?" Gail asked as Kerrigan watched her lips, painted as red as her silk blouse, move.

"Painful, but doable. I feel pain because we were each other's right hand for most of our lives. To know someone you loved to the moon and back could be so fucking heartless is beyond painful. But, walking away from you is doable because I now see exactly *who* you are. Don't get me wrong, I've seen how you've reeled people in and cut them off at the knees. I just made excuses for you. I never thought it would be me. And now I've realized losing you, losing my husband to you, is something I can survive. I no longer need or want you in my life."

"And you call me heartless?" Gail almost spat the words at her. "I don't have to listen to this. You are broken and you are taking it out on me. I saw you over there, I cannot imagine the pain you're in. I just wanted to see you, and tell you goodbye. Is that so heartless of me?"

"Broken. That's a nice way to put it." Kerrigan said,

not standing too far away from the only best friend she had ever known. "I hope you never know this kind of pain." Kerrigan meant those words. She wouldn't wish the loss of a child, a baby, on anyone.

Gail had sympathy in her eyes, or at least that is what Kerrigan assumed, until she spoke. "I wanted you to hear this from me. Keith doesn't even know yet, but since you're leaving and supposedly never coming back, I want you to know I'm pregnant." Gail spat those words out as if she was talking about the weather. It didn't even faze her, didn't even occur to her what hearing that news would do to Kerrigan.

Kerrigan stood there, feeling her knees grow weaker and become shaky. *A baby. Keith was going to have another baby. Already. Just like that.* Her face lost color and her head felt light. "You're what? I've barely been gone a month…" Kerrigan's mind was reeling. *Was this baby even Keith's? How could he be given another baby so soon, so quickly, so easily?* It may never be that easy for Kerrigan. Getting pregnant with Piper was nothing short of a miracle.

"I know my own body. I took an early pregnancy test and it was positive, immediately." Gail was not even trying to be sympathetic to Kerrigan's loss, and her pain which was still too raw.

"I hope it's a boy," Kerrigan said, watching Gail's eyes.

"Because of Piper?" Gail asked her.

"No, because a little girl with you as a mother would only learn how to grow up to be a bitch!" Before the words completely rolled off of Kerrigan's tongue, she moved closer to Gail, raised her hand in the air, and slapped her across the face. The red mark, a perfect handprint, left on the side of Gail's face had to sting because Kerrigan's hand was on fire.

Kerrigan left Gail standing there with exactly what she deserved as she got back into her jeep and barely gave the engine time to turn over before she peeled out, left the rocks fly, and left Gail Boyd in the dust.

She could have cried over this news, but she didn't. With every passing mile behind her, all of the hurt and all of the toxic feelings inside of her seemed to fade. The past was behind her now. Her new life awaited, and Kerrigan was going to embrace it with everything she had. Because that's how Kerrigan Ross lives, and loves.

Chapter 16

The last five hours of driving back to Orange Beach were rough for Kerrigan. It was three o'clock in the morning when she parked her jeep at the beach. She was hungry, but so overtired she wanted nothing else but to fall into bed. The boxes crammed inside of her jeep would have to wait. She wasn't about to make multiple trips in the dark and through the sand to unload now. The area was safe. *She was parked next to a police car, for God's sake.* Kerrigan smiled at the thought of being close to Nate again. And she was still thinking about him when she stripped down to her bra and underwear, pulled back the duvet and sheet on the bed and crawled in to get some much-needed rest.

***

It was twelve hours later before Kerrigan moved from the position she had fallen fast asleep in. Her bedroom was bright as the afternoon sun was beating through the window blinds she had left open while she was gone. Kerrigan raised her arms above her head and stretched. This house on the beach felt like home to her, and it was good to be back there.

After she showered, drank a Diet Coke, and ate a piece of dry toast – because her refrigerator was empty again – Kerrigan put on another pair of size fourteen shorts which she had thrown into her overnight bag with her toothbrush. These were a pair of stone-washed khakis with a flat front. She liked feeling a little less chunky and she felt determined again to walk the beach, daily. She found a hot-pink EMT t-shirt in the closet and slipped on her flip flops before she trekked to her jeep to begin unloading all of the boxes. Nate's police car was gone and she assumed he was at work. It seemed quiet over at Hallie's house. Kerrigan had checked on her twice while she was in Baltimore and each time Hallie's voice had sounded stronger on the phone and she insisted she felt great.

Kerrigan just kept piling up the boxes along the wall in the living room and she was about halfway finished unloading her jeep when she heard Hallie's voice holler at her. "It's about damn time you came back!" Hallie said, leaning her forearms on the railing of her deck, as Kerrigan was walking off of her own deck to make another trip to the jeep.

"I agree!" Kerrigan yelled back at her as she tried to keep herself from racing through the sand, up onto Hallie's deck, and into her arms. Hallie looked healthy and as round as ever as Kerrigan hugged her in her chocolate brown muumuu with those Birkenstocks on her feet. Kerrigan's face got close to Hallie's white hair and she instantly smelled cigarette smoke. It was the first time she had, and she remembered the doctor's warning in the hospital.

"How's the cough?" Kerrigan asked her, backing out of her arms.

"Oh the same, comes and goes," Hallie replied.

"I'm sure it helps to inhale a cig or two – and don't you try to deny it because I can smell it on you!" Kerrigan tried to scold her and Hallie just shook her head and laughed out loud. "I missed my keeper," she kidded. "I hope you found what you needed in Baltimore." Hallie meant closure, and Kerrigan nodded her head.

"I spent all of my time with my now ex-husband. We are on good terms. He is a good man who deserves to be happy. I just don't know if my once-upon-a-time-best friend can give him that." Kerrigan didn't tell Hallie how Gail claimed she's pregnant with Keith's child already. She didn't want to go there.

"You can't worry about his happiness, you need to worry about your own." Hallie said, beginning to cough with her hand balled into a fist, in front of her mouth.

"You got that right." Kerrigan said, smiling at her and thinking her cough sounded worse, maybe tighter. "I went to the cemetery. I wasn't going to, but Keith told me our baby's headstone is in place."

"That's the biggest mistake I ever made!" Hallie blurted out and Kerrigan just looked at her. "My girls are buried in Mobile, about fifty miles from here. I went there one time soon after their deaths and I swore I never would again. Too damn painful for this old woman."

"It has nothing to do with age, Hallie," Kerrigan said. "Being there, forced all of my pain to come rushing back on the spot. It was just too much and I won't go back there again either."

"You will heal on the surface, honey, but that open wound deep down inside of you, at your very core, will always bleed." Kerrigan watched Hallie reach inside of her dress to find a folded up tissue inside of her bra and she dabbed the tears seeping out of the sides of her eyes.

"It's comforting to know I'm not the only one who thinks cemeteries are for the birds!" Kerrigan said, with the intent to make Hallie laugh. Sometimes they both needed extra help gliding through their separate tragedies which have brought them unbearable sadness.

Hallie sat on her deck and watched Kerrigan make three more trips back and forth to her jeep to unload the boxes. She offered to help Kerrigan unpack them inside the beach house and that is when Kerrigan told her mostly all of the contents in the boxes were for storage. Kerrigan told her about the baby clothes, trying not to make herself sad again. Then she changed the subject to how the beach house was only her temporary home for the summer, so she needed to keep a lot of her other possessions packed up. Little did Kerrigan know, that fact saddened Hallie beyond words. She didn't want to see Kerrigan move at summer's end.

***

When Hallie went inside to rest in her recliner chair for a little while, Kerrigan decided to leave the boxes piled up in her living room and go for an evening walk on the beach. When she got out to her deck, she saw that little red sports car pull up and park next to her jeep. Bryn got out, in her tight, short shorts and another revealing tank top, and Kerrigan watched her carry a crock-pot into Nate's house. She left herself in again and this time she didn't immediately come back out. Kerrigan could see what she was up to. She wanted Nate back.

She went for her walk and when she returned, she saw Nate's squad car parked alongside of Bryn's red sports car. He was home from work and she was there with him now.

Kerrigan was not going to stoop to Bryn's level. She was not going to go over there and make a fool of herself. Nate had to have seen her jeep and know she was back. He could be the one to come see her. Kerrigan knew she was the one with the greater need in her marriage and she refused to allow herself to feel like that again with another man. She wanted him to want her and need her. It wouldn't work any other way this time, for Kerrigan.

***

Kerrigan had dinner with Hallie. She had not planned to, but decided to when she walked over to check on Hallie and she found her with her head inside of the freezer, trying to choose which TV dinner to put in the oven for herself.

"Not tonight," Kerrigan told her. "You're coming with me."

The two of them took a drive into town and ate salads and shared a pizza. It wasn't a fancy restaurant as Hallie never changed out of her muu-muu and Kerrigan was still wearing the shorts and t-shirt she put on when she woke up this afternoon. It was getting dark by the time the two of them returned from their dinner and a drive through the city. Hallie seemed to be tuckered out, but happy, as the two of them hooked arms and walked through the sand toward their beach houses. There was light at Nate's place and he opened the front door just as the two of them were walking by.

"Well, it's about time you two ladies get home…it's almost past curfew." Nate smiled at both of them as he walked the length of his deck to meet them, standing in the sand.

"My girl took me out for a pizza tonight," Hallie said, and Kerrigan was touched by her word choice. She did feel like *her girl*. "I haven't had a goddamn pizza that good in years. Those frozen ones just aren't the same." Nate smiled. "No they're not, Hallie. I'm glad Kerrigan took you out. It's good to have you back, by the way," Nate said, looking directly at Kerrigan and she didn't know how to feel. She knew how she wanted to feel, but that required someone fearless. And Kerrigan still felt doubtful and scared.

"I'm going in to get ready for bed," Hallie said as she began to waddle away from Kerrigan and Nate.

"Wait, I can walk you in," Kerrigan offered.

"I've got it," Hallie said, waving her hand in the air, without turning back as she continued on her way. "You two spend some time together. And if you want my advice…" Hallie raised her voice as she reached the steps to her deck and held on to the railing, "Hold tight to the good while you can because there is just too much bullshit in life that can come along and fuck it all up."

Nate and Kerrigan giggled at Hallie. "That sweet old woman sure does cuss like a sailor," Nate said, laughing and Kerrigan nodded her head and giggled.

"So, I can ask you right here how your trip home was or I can invite you in for a glass of wine," Nate said, hoping Kerrigan was ready to share what happened when she returned to Baltimore. He didn't want to push her, because he knew when she left she was looking for closure before she could move on.

"Are you alone?" Kerrigan asked him.

"In my house? Yes." Nate answered her, knowing she had seen his ex-wife come and go.

"Nate, I know Bryn has been hanging around – without Meggie. Are you ready to tell me what that's about?" Kerrigan looked at him, really looked at him and she could see something different in his eyes.

"I don't want to talk about this out here, please, come inside." Kerrigan walked with him into his house. He never poured any wine, he just started talking as they sat down on the couch in his dim-lit living room.

"I want to hear about your trip first," Nate said, taking her hand into his. I need to know if you're okay. I hated knowing how difficult that must have been for you."

So the subject of Bryn had to wait. Kerrigan allowed him to continue holding her hand as she spoke. "I stayed at the house with Keith. It's for sale now. He and I packed up and divided everything. I don't want to say it was nice to spend that time with him, because it was so painful for both of us. But, together, we found closure. I signed the divorce papers before I left. And you know what? That wasn't so difficult, not even close to the pain I felt packing up Piper's nursery." Nate squeezed her hand and pulled her toward him. He held her in his arms for the longest time before either of them spoke.

"My run-in with Gail didn't go near as smoothly," Kerrigan admitted, as she continued to explain, "but I survived and I don't plan to see her ever again."

"Then don't go back to Baltimore," Nate said.

"I have no intention of ever returning," Kerrigan replied.

"Really, for sure? What happens at the end of summer when MJ comes back to her place?" Nate asked.

"There are other homes or apartments in this city or anywhere else but Baltimore. I don't plan to go too far. I want to be close to Hallie," Kerrigan said.

"Anyone else you want to be close to?" Nate asked her.

"Yes, Meggie," she answered. "How is that sweet girl?" Nate smiled softly before he looked away from Kerrigan. It was that look from him again. Something appeared different.

"Kerrigan," Nate began, "Meggie is going to be staying with me more than just on weekends for awhile."

"That's wonderful!" Kerrigan said, but she noticed Nate did not seem overjoyed.

"She needs me," Nate said. "She needs both me and her mother right now." Kerrigan took a deep breath. She wondered if this was Nate's way of telling her he wanted to do right by his child and reunite with her mother so they could be a family again. She had no right to interfere in their family, Kerrigan began to tell herself. *Prepare yourself. Be strong. This never was meant to be. This man. This wonderful man is not yours to keep.* Kerrigan watched Nate's eyes fill with tears. She never said a word, he was obviously pained by having to let her go.

"Meggie is sick," he began, and Kerrigan immediately felt her heart sink as she interrupted, "What kind of sick?" *Dear God, please, let that sweet girl be okay.*

"She was just diagnosed with diabetes. Bryn caught

some warning signs and took her to be checked," Nate told her, keeping his voice low and trying very hard not to break down. He had done enough crying the past two days.

"What kind of warning signs, and what type of diabetes?" Kerrigan wanted to ask if she would need insulin for the rest of her life for Type 1, or if she had the more manageable Type 2. Kerrigan's medical background benefited her. She was good at understanding most diseases and conditions. She was one of those people who didn't go far enough into the medical field. She made a wonderful paramedic, but she could have become a fantastic doctor.

"I don't understand it all, I was not there when the doctor explained it, but Bryn told me she has Type 2, which she will not need insulin for, but she does have to take some type of medicine. Some of the warning signs were her constant thirst and need to pee." The times Kerrigan has been with Meggie at length, she had not once noticed either of those things. "Well, that is good, Nate. If Meggie has to have one of the two, she has the better one, in my opinion. But..." Kerrigan hesitated to continue.

"But, what?"

"I don't think it's my place to say this..."

"You have a place, believe me, you do." Nate reassured her and she smiled at him.

"Have you ever noticed those warning signs in Meggie?" Kerrigan asked him.

"To be honest, no," Nate replied. "I just thought I

didn't pay enough attention. I mean, at first when Bryn told me Meggie has diabetes, I lost it and immediately blamed all the candy she eats. Apparently, the two aren't related unless a child is obese and sugar intake has led to the weight gain and the diabetes. I don't know, as I said, I don't understand all of this. It's like it came out of nowhere and I just want my little girl back, and whole again." He put his face in his hands, and Kerrigan felt her own heart breaking for him. For his pain.

She pulled him close and held him while he regained his composure. "She will make it through this. She will adapt to whatever lifestyle she needs to, in order to stay healthy. Some kids with Type 2 are able to lower their blood sugar levels and eventually even stop taking diabetes medicine if they eat right and exercise as they grow." Kerrigan wanted more information, but Nate couldn't give it to her. This was all still new and too fresh, and hearing everything secondhand from Bryn obviously had not given him the clarity he needs.

"How do you know so much?" Nate asked her, as he realized her background as a former emergency medical technician, but still remained impressed with her medical knowledge.

"It's my thing," she answered and he smiled at her.

"You are the first person to make me feel better about this," Nate said, sighing. "Bryn is so dramatic and pessimistic, and she just keeps bringing me down with her."

"Well, we can't have that," Kerrigan replied, giving him a soft smile. "I think you need to go along to Meggie's next doctor's appointment. Ask questions, get educated, it's your job as her daddy to help her in every way you can and you can't do that if you don't understand what she is dealing with."

"I will," he said. "Thank you for being here for me." Kerrigan wanted to say she wouldn't want be anywhere else right now, but she held back. She knew Meggie's condition was bound to bring Bryn back into Nate's life, front and center. That sweet little girl needed both of her parents now, and Kerrigan was not sure where that left her. She felt like she had been pushed to the sidelines. And, maybe, now she would have to willingly take herself out of the game.

Chapter 17

Kerrigan tossed and turned in her bed, hours after Nate told her about Meggie. It saddened her, and it pained her to watch Nate struggle with knowing his little girl was not healthy. She was thinking of Piper again, still, but especially tonight. Diseases, diagnosis, crisis, problems and scary moments come up for every parent and with any child. But, losing a child – a brand new baby – before even being given a chance felt beyond unfair. She could have handled anything, anything at all, if Piper had stayed with her. Kerrigan sat up in bed, crying as she reached for the yellow blanket she kept in her bed all of the time now. The scent of her baby had faded. Gone. Just like Piper. Kerrigan hoped she would never forget what Piper looked like. She didn't want that memory to disappear. She wanted her mind to always be able to take her there, to imagine her baby's face, her features. She and Keith had taken so many photographs of their baby, and Kerrigan still had those saved in her cell phone.

She reached onto the nightstand by the bed to pick up her phone. She selected the gallery of photographs. Those were the last ones she had taken, and there were well over two hundred pictures. Her high forehead, round face, and small chin reminded Kerrigan of Keith's. Her dark blue eyes and her nose and her mouth were tiny replicas of Kerrigan's. This was the first time she had the courage to look at those pictures. She wanted to keep them forever, of course, but it pained her to see something, someone so real in pictures, right in front of her, knowing she was gone forever.

The tears kept flowing with each photograph and Kerrigan found herself in that quicksand again. The feeling of sinking deeper and deeper into a pit of sadness and of wonder. Wondering why in the world God lets things like that happen. Wondering if her baby would be waiting for her in heaven one day. And if she was, will Piper still be a baby, or would she grow with each passing year?

"Why am I here, God? What am I supposed to do now?" Kerrigan asked aloud in her dark bedroom. "I lost everything and just when I began to believe you may have a plan for me here, with Hallie and with Nate and sweet Meggie, I find myself feeling like I don't belong. Meggie's sick and she needs both of her parents, together. I can't be in the way of any chance for that to happen. You supposedly have all of answers, so tell me what to do…" She never bowed her head in prayer, she just spoke those words outright and aloud in private. *Close enough to a prayer,* Kerrigan thought, as she was startled by her cell phone ringing in her hand. It was two o'clock in the morning, and Keith was calling her.

Kerrigan didn't hesitate to answer. *Something had to be wrong.* "Hello? Keith?"

"Kerrie, I'm sorry to wake you…" His voice sounded calm.

"You didn't. I'm having a hard time sleeping.…I keep thinking about her." It felt easy to admit that to him now. "What about you, are you okay?"

"I'm okay," he answered, but Kerrigan didn't believe him.

"Then why are you calling me in the middle of the night?" Kerrigan felt herself smiling into the phone.

"Because I miss my best friend…" His answer surprised her.

"See, I told you, we made much better friends than lovers," she said, waiting for him to say more after she heard him laugh softly on the opposite end of the phone.

"I feel so guilty, Kerrie…" Kerrigan listened for more. "I am in love with Gail, I'm happy with her, I want a life with her." Kerrigan closed her eyes while she held the phone up to her ear. This was not the easiest for her to hear. *Just move on, but leave me out of it.* "And now… she's pregnant with my baby." Kerrigan wanted to blurt out, *I already know that!* But, instead, she thought before she spoke. "Keith…just be happy," she said, softly, and swallowing hard in hopes of pushing that lump back down her throat. "Don't feel guilty for creating a baby. You know what a gift that is. Appreciate every damn second, promise me you will, and when your baby is here – be the kind of daddy I know you are." By now, both Kerrigan and Keith were crying on the phone.

"Do you think we will ever see her again?" Keith asked, choking back his tears.

"I hope so," Kerrigan answered, realizing she had just been questioning God about the very same thing. "Keith, listen to me. If you can find what it is you're supposed to be here for, in this life, hold onto it." Keith knew she meant both Gail and their blessing on the way. What Keith did not know was that Kerrigan had been given the answer she asked God for just moments ago. Her advice to Keith, the advice which freely rolled off of her tongue, were the same words she too needed to take to heart. *If you can find what it is you're supposed to be here for, in this life, hold onto it.*

Their phone conversation ended a short time later, and before three o'clock, Kerrigan was up, out of bed, wearing a white, fleece robe with only her cotton underwear underneath, and she was sitting outside in the dark on her deck. She already had a Diet Coke open. Listening to the ocean waves relaxed her. This was where she was supposed to be right now. She wanted to be with Hallie, to take care of her. She was a tough, stubborn, old woman who could most certainly take care of herself, but Kerrigan liked being with her and being there for her. And then there's Nate. Could Kerrigan really sit back and watch his ex-wife reclaim him, and probably hurt him again? He deserved better. He deserved to be loved without any doubts or questions. Kerrigan wanted that chance to love him, she was certain of it now.

***

Kerrigan waited for the sun to come up and she walked the beach for over an hour. She was feeling good when she returned to the beach house and took a shower before she decided to scramble some eggs for herself and for Hallie. She divided up the eggs and two pieces of dry toast on two plates and immediately walked over to Hallie's. She didn't knock, she just tried to gracefully juggle the two plates of food as she opened her door. The living room was quiet and dark as the window blinds were still closed from the night before. It was unusual for Hallie to sleep in, and Kerrigan felt uneasy as she called out for her and heard no answer. She immediately set both of the plates of food down on the coffee table in front of the couch, and she accidently knocked over a picture frame while doing so. All of those tables, cluttered with photos. Her family. Her memories.

As Kerrigan rushed down the short hallway, she called for Hallie again. The bathroom was empty and then she saw her lying in bed, on her back, covered up to her chin, eyes closed. Kerrigan froze. She thought of Piper. She thought of that dreadful moment when she found her lifeless. This could not be happening to her again!

Kerrigan put both of her hands on the sides of Hallie's face. She felt warm. Too warm. And she startled her awake. "For the love of God!" Hallie barked in a voice that sounded hoarse and cut in and out because she had not been fully awake. "Oh, Hallie, I'm sorry to scare you, but you scared me! It's late morning and you're still sleeping and I brought breakfast, and oh thank God, you're okay!"

Kerrigan sat on the side of the bed and threw herself onto Hallie's chest and she cried. Hallie just held her. She knew Kerrigan was haunted by the memory of losing her baby in her sleep.

A few minutes later, Kerrigan apologized again as she backed away from Hallie. She stood up from the bed and wiped the tears off of her face with her t-shirt sleeve as Hallie sat up in bed. She had a sleeveless white cotton nightgown on with a scoop neck, and Kerrigan noticed obvious pulsations in her neck veins. "It's okay, honey. Sit back down. We need to talk."

Kerrigan sat on the bed next to her again as Hallie reached for her hand. "My health is not going to be much better than it is right now, it's only going to decline. I am old, and it's okay. I want to see my family. I'm ready to see my family."

"No!" Kerrigan reacted, abruptly. "Are you giving up? You never sleep until ten a.m.! Hallie, I need you here. I just found you, for chrissakes."

"You didn't find me. I barged in and annoyed your ass." Hallie grinned at her.

"I mean it," Kerrigan said, seriously. "I just found you. I want you to hear this. You have been missing all my life. I've never had a real mother. I know you could be my grandmother, but you fill a void inside of my heart like a mother should." Kerrigan had tears in her eyes as she spoke. Suddenly she was terrified to lose this old woman.

"And you have done much of the same, for me," Hallie spoke softly, and then she stopped to cough with her balled fist covering her mouth. "I lost my girls, and now I have you. You're my fourth daughter. I truly believe God sent you, to me."

"I love you, Hallie." Kerrigan said it first.

"And I love you, honey." Neither of them cried, as they sat there holding hands on the bed for endless minutes until Kerrigan told her she brought breakfast, but it's probably cold by now.

"Let's get you out of bed and I will heat our plates in the kitchen," Kerrigan suggested as she pulled the covers back from Hallie's lower half. Her eyes immediately went to Hallie's legs. They were bare, because she was only wearing a nightgown and they were obviously swollen.

"Hallie, your legs…how long have they been like that?" Kerrigan asked her.

"A day or so," she answered. "I've probably been on my feet too much." Kerrigan knew better. She knew Hallie's routine. She relaxed in the sun. She relaxed inside. Even her time spent cooking had lessened since her scare with a collapsed lung. Again, Kerrigan's medical instincts kicked in and she put together how the pulsating veins in her neck and the swollen legs were warning signs for poor circulation. She knew how chronic lung damage can prevent the heart from circulating blood normally.

"Let's get you dressed, you need to go to the

hospital," Kerrigan said, as she attempted to help Hallie up out of bed and get her undressed.

"Oh, honey, please I am not an invalid," Hallie said, standing up on her own beside the bed. "And, besides, you don't wanna see me in the buff." Kerrigan smiled at her and replied, "Oh you've seen one ass, you've seen 'em all!" They both giggled. With Kerrigan's help, Hallie managed to wash her face, brush her teeth and put on a clean muu-muu, this one powder blue. As Kerrigan helped her slip into her Birckenstocks, she noticed her feet were swollen too. "We need to get going, Hallie," Kerrigan said, feeling worried. She appeared weak and nervous about needing so much assistance. "Are you sure you will not let me call for an ambulance?"

"You are my ambulance," Hallie said, insisting she did not want to be hauled away in a rush with the sirens blaring again.

As Kerrigan helped Hallie make her way down the deck and into the sand, she looked over at Nate's house. This time of day she knew he was at work. She wanted him to know about Hallie, but she didn't have a chance to call him now. She would let him know later.

***

Kerrigan drove equally as fast as an emergency vehicle would have, but she was experienced with handling that kind of pressure and when she and Hallie arrived at the hospital's emergency room, Kerrigan was able to relay as much detail to the medical personnel on staff as any paramedic. And then she was asked to have a seat in the waiting area while they tended to Hallie.

She sat down and tried not to look around at the other people with worried or shocked faces. She didn't want to be alone while she waited, so she called Nate. He had just as much right as she did to be there. For Hallie.

His cell phone rang twice before he picked up. "Kerrigan?"

"Are you busy?" she asked.

"I'm about three hours away, transporting a prisoner to the penitentiary," he told her as the reception on his cell phone cut out and came back again. "Everything okay?"

"Yes, I'm fine. Just wanted to talk. Call me after you're back tonight, okay?" Kerrigan didn't want to worry him or make him feel pressured into being there. She told herself she could handle this by herself. *Hallie will be okay.*

"I will, and Kerrigan..."

"Yes?"

"This is the first time you've called me...and I like it. I like knowing you thought about me. I guess what I'm trying to say is thanks, you just made my day." Kerrigan could hear a smile in his voice. She wished he was there because she wanted to pull him close and never let him go.

"You're welcome," she replied, "I like it, too."

As she ended her call, a nurse peeked her head out of the sliding window at the patient check-in desk and asked Kerrigan to follow her. When she saw Hallie lying in a hospital bed, hooked up to oxygen, Kerrigan looked at the doctor in the room for answers.

"You got her here in good time," a doctor who looked to be in his mid-fifties with graying short black hair and a slim build, said to Kerrigan. "She's definitely dealing with pulmonary hypertension."

The doctor proceeded to tell both Hallie and Kerrigan how there was no cure for that, just as there was no cure for her emphysema. But, he wanted to prescribe yet another medicine for Hallie, this one would relax the blood vessels in her lungs and reduce excess cell growth in the blood vessels. As the blood vessels relax, the doctor explained, more blood would flow through them. Kerrigan already knew that, so she jumped ahead of the doctor and asked about the risk of blood clots. She was worried Hallie's body would try to compensate for the low oxygen by increasing its number of red blood cells, and sometimes that severity caused the blood to clot. The doctor told Hallie she had to stay overnight for periodic blood work and observation for that very reason.

Hallie balked and Kerrigan insisted. And less than an hour later, Hallie was admitted and received a private room. Kerrigan sat with her for the entire day, watching her sleep and talking to her as she drifted in and out of her rested state. She had not eaten much off of the dinner tray in front of her when she asked to lay back and rest again. Kerrigan helped her get comfortable and sat back down in the chair beside her bed.

"Honey..." Hallie said hoarsely with her eyes looking heavy.

"Yes?"

"You need to go back to the beach. Don't wear your ass out sitting here all night long in that hardback chair. Go get some good rest and come back for me tomorrow." Hallie could see how worried Kerrigan was feeling, so she added, "I'm not going anywhere. I'm not ready to check out...just yet." She winked and Kerrigan stood up abruptly from her chair and took Hallie's hand into her own. "You better not be."

Chapter 18

It was the stress built up from sitting in the hospital all day, the uncertainty of how much time Hallie had left, and the fear of losing her. All of it came to its boiling over point as Kerrigan stood in the sand very near the ocean as the waves rushed up to her, meeting her lower legs. The wind picked up as Kerrigan stood under the evening sky with tears escaping down her cheeks.

She never even heard him come up from behind her, until he spoke her name. She turned around to find Nate, still in his work clothes with his police badge visible, hanging from the left side of his belt, and he was barefoot in his jeans, knowing he would get his feet wet standing that close to the water with Kerrigan. "I just got back," he said, noticing her tears. "I'm here now, talk to me." Kerrigan fell into his arms. He knew she was still in so much pain from losing her baby, so he just held onto her for as long as she needed him to. And when she pulled out of his arms, she surprised him with her words.

"It's Hallie…she's declining." Kerrigan explained to Nate what happened and how Hallie was in the hospital again. He listened with concern in his eyes and his heart, too, felt heavy. He wasn't ready to lose Hallie either.

Kerrigan felt like crying again as the two of them walked back to the beach houses. "I want you to hold on to any little bit of hope you have left inside of you," Nate told Kerrigan as they reached her deck first.

"What do you mean by that?" she asked.

"You've lost so damn much, I can't imagine a sliver of hope left inside of your heart, but I'm asking you to find what's left and hold onto what's there with everything you have. Believe Hallie has more time…and believe me when I tell you that I love you. I love you for who you are. You're real. You inspire me to be better at handling the shit life throws at me. You've been beaten down in the worst way and you've clawed your way back because you want to live again. Give some of that fight to Hallie. She needs it now, she needs you, and so do I." Kerrigan's eyes widened as Nate bent down on one knee in front of her.

She wanted to say *what in the hell are you doing* but she couldn't speak the words. She just watched him kneeling before her. "This isn't a marriage proposal," Nate said with a lopsided grin on his face and Kerrigan actually let out a giggle. She felt relieved and a little confused at the same time. "I didn't plan this," Nate continued, "but I'm asking you to love me and need and want me as much as I do you." Kerrigan took the hand he reached out to her and she momentarily closed her eyes and opened them again as she spoke. "Nate Stein, I already love you, and you have no idea how much I need and want you."

"Forever? he asked her.

"It's a definite maybe," Kerrigan said, smiling at him. She was not crying. She was entirely too fulfilled and happy at this moment to cry as she watched him jump to his feet and pull her into his big, strong arms, and then he took her face into both of his hands as he pressed his lips to hers and kissed her hard and full on the mouth.

The two of them were into their moment, feeling like they could overcome anything that lies ahead, as long as they have each other. And that was when Bryn interrupted them.

"Really, Nate? Meggie does not need to see this." Nate and Kerrigan separated from each other's arms as Bryn continued to react. "I thought we were going have dinner together. Meggie is already inside." Kerrigan knew Bryn must have seen Nate on one knee in front of her just moments ago. While he did not officially propose marriage to her, he committed himself to Kerrigan and she accepted him.

"What Meggie sees between me and Kerrigan is our business, not yours," Nate responded and Kerrigan managed to keep a straight face while staring at Bryn.

"We have a lot to work out before you make life-changing plans with her, or anyone." Bryn only looked at Nate. It was as if she was pretending Kerrigan was not even there, and Kerrigan suddenly felt in control. It was time to for this ex-wife to act like an ex-wife and stop meddling. *Back off*. Kerrigan had a place in Nate's life now.

"We share a child, Bryn. You and I are friends, that's all," Nate said. "Who I spend my time with…and who I fall in love with really should not concern you anymore." Bryn's eyes widened as Nate reached for Kerrigan's hand and pulled her with him up onto her deck and they walked into Kerrigan's house. Before Nate closed the door, he looked back at Bryn and told her to tell Meggie he would see her in a few minutes.

Bryn stormed through the sand and back into Nate's house as Nate stood close to Kerrigan behind the closed door in her living room. "Don't let her get to you," he said.

"I didn't," Kerrigan assured him. "Thank you for being so honest out there. I know you care about her, I know she has confused you lately, but what you said about me…"

"I meant it," Nate interrupted. "I've fallen in love with you, and I've fallen hard." He smiled at her and kissed her. She kissed him back and he led her down onto the couch. Their passion quickly escalated, but came to an abrupt halt when the door opened up and Meggie was standing there.

"That's what mommy and Jenny do sometimes," she said as she watched Nate and Kerrigan quickly separate.

"Hey, baby girl." Nate walked over to her and picked her up. "I'll bet you're hungry and I'll also bet that your mommy sent you over here to get me."

"Uh huh," Meggie replied as she nodded her head, and then Kerrigan walked over to her. "How are you feeling, sweet girl?"

"Good." Meggie responded. "Are you going to eat hamburgers with us tonight?" Kerrigan looked at Nate and he said, "You're welcome to join us. Meggie likes hamburgers, so I'm grilling tonight."

"Bring me one later," Kerrigan said, smiling at him and then back at Meggie. "And, you, I want you to come see me the next time your mommy drops you off at your daddy's house. We need some girl time." Kerrigan brushed away a red curl from Meggie's forehead.

"Okay, but I can't eat any more candy with you," Meggie said, seriously.

"Alright, no candy." Kerrigan agreed and felt sorry for Meggie. It had to be difficult for her to understand how her body now needed special care.

When the two of them left, Kerrigan felt optimistic again. She wanted to be a part of their lives. She wanted to share her life with them. *Someday soon.*

***

Kerrigan called the hospital to check on Hallie, and the nurse told her she was resting comfortably and her red blood cell count had not escalated. That news meant Hallie would be discharged tomorrow. Kerrigan was looking forward to bringing her back to the beach again.

It was two o'clock in the morning when Kerrigan was startled by her cell phone ringing next to her bed. She reached for it on the nightstand and accidentally knocked it onto the floor. It rang two more times before she grabbed ahold of it and answered.

She tried to come to her senses as she said hello. She had been in a deep sleep. She remembered falling asleep after giving up on waiting for Nate to come over following his late dinner with Meggie...and Bryn. He never showed and he never called. She assumed it was him calling now but the phone was pressed against her ear before she looked at the caller's name.

"Is this Kerrigan Ross?" The voice was unfamiliar to her.

"Yes it is," she said sounding exactly as she felt. Half asleep.

"This is Tammy Varel, I'm a nurse at Diercks Hospital. I think you should get here. There's been a sudden change."

She was already in her bra and underwear and began throwing on the rest of her clothes, just shorts and a t-shirt again, as she grabbed her phone and found her car keys on the kitchen table and flip flops by the couch as she rushed out of the door. It was dark on the beach and the air felt cool on her bare arms, legs, and feet as she quickly made her way through the sand and past Hallie's house and then Nate's. She wondered why he never came by last night, and when she got into her jeep and began to back out of her parking spot, she realized why. She saw Bryn's little red sports car still parked there. She stayed the night with Nate.

***

Kerrigan didn't know the highways of Orange Beach all too well, but she did know how to get to the hospital. Her two trips there, in only two months since she moved to Orange Beach, had been with Hallie. She was scared now as she entered the sliding glass doors of the hospital's main entrance. It might have helped at this moment for Kerrigan to send up a prayer, but she couldn't do it. She was so fearful God had taken another person from her.

She made her way up to the nurse's desk on the second floor. She didn't recognize any of the staff on duty because the shift changed since she was there during the daytime hours. One of the nurses saw Kerrigan and made eye contact with her. Kerrigan was surprised to see Jenny, Bryn's girlfriend, wearing pale yellow scrubs and staring back at her. "Jenny?" Kerrigan did not know she was a nurse. She had no idea what Bryn did for a living either. "Hi," Jenny replied. "You're here for Hallie?"

"I got a call from a nurse, I think she said her name was Tammy…I rushed over here…please tell me what is going on."

"Hallie flatlined earlier," Jenny began to explain and Kerrigan held herself up with her hands on the counter in front of her. "She's still with us, but her heart is weak. You should go in there."

When Kerrigan walked into Hallie's hospital room, she expected to find her asleep but the light was on and a nurse was in there with her. "Hallie…" Kerrigan said walking up to her bedside. Hallie looked tired and pale. Her face blended too well with her snow-white hair. Gone was the bronze coloring from the sun Hallie liked to soak up on the beach. Hallie's life on the beach the past twenty-something years had not been the easiest, as she grieved and often times felt lonely, but she did love the sand, the sun, and being very near the water. It's where she found peace.

"I wanted them to call you," Hallie said, trying to speak clearly but her voice sounded terribly weak.

"I'm glad they did," Kerrigan replied, reaching for Hallie's hand and glancing at the nurse on the opposite side of Hallie's bed.

"I'm Tammy," the nurse said. "You should know Hallie had a mild heart attack about an hour ago. I don't know how familiar you are with emphysema," the nurse continued speaking, "it makes the heart work harder. It's difficult for the heart to pump blood to the lungs and it makes it harder for the lungs to oxygenate the blood." Kerrigan nodded her head. "This sets up a cycle where the heart just keeps having to work too much and damage can occur from this. Patients may end up with heart enlargement, heart failure, or a heart attack. Smoking makes this so much worse too," the nurse concluded as she shook her head at Hallie.

"Don't tell me you tried to light up in here?" Kerrigan asked, attempting to be firm, but really trying to avoid facing the frightening reality of this moment. She was going to lose this woman.

"Oh! No one is any fun around here, especially that housekeeper who I know smokes like a haystack. She wouldn't give up one goddamn cigarette to me earlier today." Hallie winked at Kerrigan and Kerrigan giggled aloud while the nurse shook her head again. She didn't quite understand Hallie's keen sense of humor and she didn't at all grasp the fact that one more laugh, a few more moments of sharing words, sharing life, was something both Kerrigan and Hallie desperately needed. Probably more so for Kerrigan than Hallie.

When the nurse walked out, Kerrigan sat down in the armchair beside Hallie's bed. "You do know what this means, don't you?" Hallie asked Kerrigan as she coughed a few times while attempting to get out the words.

"It means you have to fight like hell to live," Kerrigan replied, knowing better. This was one of those moments when she wished her medical background was nonexistent. She wanted to be naïve and believe Hallie had ten or fifteen more years of life left inside of her.

"I saw my girls earlier," Hallie said with a smile that completely lit up her eyes and brought a little color back into her cheeks.

"What?" Kerrigan felt chill bumps on her forearms.

"My heart stopped beating, I guess. I started to leave this earth. I felt myself escape this old body and I could see the doctor and nurses working on me, taking turns giving me chest compressions. It wasn't like in the movies with those paddles in their hands, trying to shock my heart back into rhythm." Kerrigan was listening raptly. She heard about stories like this before, but she never knew if they were true and she certainly had never known anyone personally who experienced dying and coming back. "I walked toward the doorway here, right over there," Hallie pointed, "and I saw them. My beautiful girls, looking like angels in their white dresses. They haven't changed a bit, just as I remember them. They told me Stanley is waiting for me, too." Hallie did not have a single tear in her eyes, just pure joy, as Kerrigan struggled to keep her composure. "I could hear a harp playing in the distance, from heaven. I wanted to keep walking toward them, to touch them and hold them, but my feet would no longer move. I could breathe so well, my lungs were good again. So good, I tried to run to my girls, but I failed with every attempt. They told me to go back and when I asked them why...they told me, *for you*."

"To be with me?" Kerrigan asked, feeling the lump in her throat and taking two of her fingers to wipe away the single tear that escaped her eye.

"No, honey...to say goodbye to you. To leave you with the strength you need to carry on, to embrace life. You are still just a girl, only twenty-eight years old. You have your whole life ahead of you. I need peace in my heart in knowing you will be better than okay." Hallie held out her hand to Kerrigan and she grabbed ahold of it in desperation.

"I can't lose you!" Kerrigan bent over the bed and cried as she felt Hallie's hand brushing back and forth on the top of her head and through the long, dark curls in her hair which she had hanging loose and down to her shoulders because it was the middle of the night when she got the call to rush to this woman's side. This woman who had come to mean the world to her.

"Kerrigan..." Hallie said, as she watched her lift up her head to look at her. "You have already been through too much in your young life. Most people could not handle loss the way you have. When I saw you for the very first time, when you came to the beach, I saw myself in you."

"Don't compare your strength to mine," Kerrigan interrupted, "I'm not half as strong as you are, Hallie."

"You're stronger," Hallie stated. "You are younger than I was when I was knocked down with horrific grief.

You have already bounced back in ways that took me years to reach. Keep moving forward, honey. You are going to have a happy, full life."

"How can you be so sure?" Kerrigan asked her, feeling overcome with sadness. She was not prepared for this.

"Because I am going to be up there calling the shots," Hallie tried to laugh but she ended up coughing. Kerrigan smiled at her as she imagined her up in heaven attempting to take over for God. It took longer this time for Hallie to clear her throat and airway again. It was becoming more difficult for her to speak, too.

"Maybe you should rest," Kerrigan suggested. "I will be right here."

"Not yet," Hallie replied. "I need you to understand."

"I do," Kerrigan tried to reassure her and she actually felt a sense of calm come over her. She knew she needed to find her strength and give Hallie her peace.

"The beach houses…" Hallie continued, "are yours. I had a lawyer draw up the papers when you were away."

"What? No…" Kerrigan said, not knowing what else to say and feeling like that was a gift entirely too generous to accept.

"Yes," Hallie said to her. "You own them now. I want to leave you with what I have left. You won't need to worry about a place to stay after MJ comes back, or your financial future for awhile." Kerrigan had absolutely no idea of Hallie's worth, nor did she care. She didn't want her real estate or her bank account. She wanted her. She needed her.

"I am at a loss for words, Hallie," Kerrigan said. "You know money and things do not mean anything to me. You know what I drive, what I wear. I'm low maintenance." Kerrigan wanted to add how she just needed *her* in her life, but she knew that was now out of their control.

"Is this your way of saying you aren't fancy enough to wear the muu-muus I'm willing to you?" Hallie laughed out loud and this time she managed not to cough, and Kerrigan giggled.

"Thank you for what you have brought to my life in such a short period of time," Kerrigan began, sincerely. "Thank you for teaching me how to laugh again, but most of all, I will always be grateful to you for showing me the way, for giving me motherly advice and motherly love. For the first time in my life, you made me feel like I belonged somewhere."

"You do belong on that beach. Be happy there, honey. And when I go, I'm taking you with me in my heart. You will always be in my heart." Kerrigan could not believe Hallie's words. Those are the very same words she said to her baby, to Piper, after she was gone. Kerrigan tried very hard not to cry as she spoke, "I told Piper that. I told her those exact words, how she is in my heart."

"From a mother…to a daughter," Hallie said, bringing a smile to Kerrigan's face. But that smile quickly faded as she watched Hallie close her eyes and the line on the heart monitor near the head of her hospital bed completely flattened. The beeping sound was alarming and seconds later two nurses rushed into the room. Kerrigan didn't know if they were going to make an attempt to bring her back again. For her own selfish reasons, Kerrigan could have jumped up and grabbed a pair of defibrillator paddles herself. She would have given her own life to save Hallie, given her both of her lungs or whatever she needed. But she knew what she had to do. For Hallie.

"It's okay. Just let her go." As Kerrigan said those words, both nurses remained in the room. Tammy turned off the machine and the room was quiet again. "I'm sorry for your loss," Jenny, with her short cropped blonde hair and small, but muscular body, said as she gently touched Kerrigan on her arm.

Kerrigan only nodded her head. *My loss. How tiring it was to keep having losses*. But, this time, what she gained from knowing and loving Hallie had given her something she had never experienced before. Maternal love. Courage to overcome grief. And the strength to survive.

Chapter 19

Kerrigan remained beside Hallie's body. She could already feel the warmth vanishing from her hand as she held it. She had asked the nurses if she could be alone with Hallie for awhile. She needed this time. And she would be forever grateful for the time she was given to talk to and say goodbye to Hallie. She had only known this woman for nine weeks, but they shared a bond and a love that many do not even find in a lifetime.

Before she was ready to leave, the door to the hospital room slowly opened and Kerrigan turned, expecting to find one of the nurses coming inside. Her eyes widened and immediately teared up when she saw Nate standing there. "Jenny called me," he said softly. "I'm so glad you were here, when she–"

"Me too," Kerrigan said, standing up in front of her chair as Nate walked swiftly toward her and enveloped her into his arms. His physical strength was exactly what she needed right now. He wrapped his arms tighter around her and she closed her eyes when she heard him say, "I will miss her, too."

Nate and Kerrigan were not given much more time alone in that hospital room with Hallie. After Nate took Hallie's hand into his and left her with a kiss, Jenny entered the room and said they must leave.

Kerrigan took a deep breath. She knew this was the last time she would see Hallie. Even though she was now looking at just a body, a shell, she wanted to stay and remember her. Her short, thick, snow-white hair, the deep wrinkles on her face that defined age and character as well as grief and loss. Those wrinkles told her story.

Kerrigan kissed Hallie on the side of her cheek, and whispered, *"I love you"* to her before she took Nate's hand, which he had held out to her, and walked away.

***

Nate drove behind Kerrigan in her jeep while they made their way back to the beach houses. As they walked together through the sand, Kerrigan was silent. "Come back to my house with me," Nate suggested and Kerrigan only nodded her head in agreement.

She sat down on his couch while he went into the kitchen and returned with a Diet Coke for her. Kerrigan smiled as she accepted the cold can from him, opened it, and took a long drink.

Nate was afraid of how another loss would affect Kerrigan. He knew she and Hallie had crossed paths for a reason, but he cursed what little time they had together. He wanted to be careful of what he said to Kerrigan now, but he also wanted to reach her before she fell in too deep in her grief again. "Kerrigan, I know the pain you're in. I feel like I did when I lost my grandmother when I was fifteen years old," Nate said, choosing his words with care. "I am here for you if you need to talk or cry or scream and holler." Kerrigan smiled at him.

"I am better than I would have been if I had not gotten there in time," Kerrigan said, "because I know she waited for me. She told the nurses to call me, because she had words for me. You know Hallie, she wasn't even going to let dying stop her from getting her point across." Nate smiled and Kerrigan managed to laugh out loud with tears in her eyes. "She gave me so much in the short time that I spent with her, and now she has left me with something I don't even feel right accepting." As Kerrigan was trying to explain to Nate how the beach houses were now hers, he stood up and walked over to open a drawer inside of his entertainment center, above the television. He pulled out a large manila envelope and came back over to sit beside her on the couch. "She knew you would feel that way. She had her affairs in order and she made some changes when you went back to Baltimore. I helped her finalize everything with a lawyer. Kerrigan, Hallie wanted, with all of her heart, for you to have the beach houses and so much more. She took care of me and Meggie in her plans, too," Nate said, "so don't you feel like you're the only special one."

He handed her the envelope and she held it on her lap before opening it. "This just seems too final," Kerrigan said as Nate agreed. And then she began to open it. She found the papers which named her as the sole owner of all three of the beach houses. Everything in Hallie's house was now Kerrigan's, too. Kerrigan was happy to know she could keep the pictures of Hallie and her family. She didn't have any pictures of her own of Hallie. Suddenly she wished she had taken a silly selfie with her at least one time. It was the little things that mattered most to Kerrigan. She read further into the document and put her hand over her mouth and looked up at Nate. He only nodded his head. He knew what kind of a woman Kerrigan was. He knew how she lived. She had never been financially secure in her independent life since college. That was going to change for her as she now had inherited nine hundred and eighty-five thousand dollars from Hallie. "I can't...I don't know what to do with almost a million dollars," Kerrigan said in astonishment and Nate giggled at her.

"You are something else, you know that?" he asked her. "I've never known anyone like you. You are an amazing woman, Kerrigan Ross."

"Hallie is the amazing one, I mean, *was*," Kerrigan sadly corrected herself. "I can't believe she loved me this much."

"We all do," Nate said, putting his arm around her shoulders and pulling her close. He gave her a kiss on the top of her head and she wrapped both of her arms around his torso. And then Kerrigan found a letter inside of the manila envelope. "What is this?" she asked, looking over at Nate.

"Probably more words of wisdom," Nate answered as he stood up. "I will leave you alone to read it. She gave me one too and told me to read it after she was gone. I didn't wait, I read it soon after she gave it to me. As you said, she was one amazing woman."

Nate walked into the kitchen as Kerrigan opened the hand-written letter. Her hands were shaky as she felt nervous to read Hallie's words. Again, this seemed too final.

Her handwriting was legible, but Kerrigan could tell it was written by an elderly person with a sometimes unsteady hand. She had never seen anything handwritten by Hallie, so even before reading what the letter said, Kerrigan already treasured what she now held in her hands.

Lori Bell

Dear Kerrigan,

There are moments in life when you know from that point forward you will never be the same. I experienced those moments a few times in my long life. When I fell in love with a man who completed me. When I became a mother for the very first time and then two more times after. And then, I felt the opposite, rippling effects of this when tragedy took my family away from me. My life has not been easy, but I chose to recognize the blessings and hold tight to each and every one. You, Kerrigan, were my final blessing in this life. We were placed in each other's paths for a reason. You have so much to give and so much life inside of you. Don't succumb to sadness. Feel it, and then move on to what makes you shine. You were the sun in my life on this beach for the remaining few months of my life. Now, go, be the sun in the lives of others. If Nate is the man you love, then dammit, seize a future with him. Stanley used to look at me the way Nate looks at you. If that is not real love, well, I'll bet my selection of muu-muus it is. This is just me relishing in telling you what to do one last time. Live. Love. Laugh. Be who you are. Life is too fucking short not to be happy.

I love you as my own, my fourth and beautiful daughter.

Hallie

Chapter 20

Two days later, Kerrigan was standing on the shore with Meggie on her left, Nate on her right, and Hallie's ashes in the urn she held in her arms.

"This is where she wanted to be," Kerrigan said, looking out at the ocean waves. It was seven o'clock on Saturday morning, only three days since Hallie's life ended.

"She didn't want to be in a cemetery?" Meggie asked.

"No, she didn't. Remember how she used to talk about her girls being buried there?"

"And her Stanley, too!" Meggie stated. For four and a half years old, she had it together, Kerrigan thought as she smiled at Meggie in her lime green sundress and flip flops to match. "Yes, her husband, too," Kerrigan agreed.

"Why doesn't she want to be with them?" Meggie asked as Nate waited for Kerrigan to explain. The two of them had already talked about how both Hallie and Kerrigan felt about loved ones being buried in the cemetery. It was just too painful to imagine a loved one under the ground. Kerrigan wanted to carry out Hallie's wishes to be cremated and have her ashes spread at the edge of the shore and carried away by the ocean waves.

"She is with them, in heaven, Meggie," Kerrigan began to explain. "And she wanted what was left of her body here on earth to be with the ocean. This was her home for many years after she lost her family. This is where she found some peace and tried to heal her heart."

"I want to see Hallie, again," Meggie said, and Kerrigan responded, "I do, too, and we will again someday. Right now, she is busy reuniting with her family and I know she is so happy and she wants us to not be so sad that she died, okay?" Meggie nodded her head as Kerrigan knelt down in the sand beside her. She set down the urn and took the lid off. It was a windy day and some of the ashes blew out and onto Meggie's feet. Her little eyes widened and she immediately ran closer to the water to catch the waves on her feet as they washed the ashes off and carried them out to sea. Nate looked at Kerrigan and the two of them shared a smile. As the rest of Hallie's ashes were washed away, the three of them stood there in the sand, holding hands in silence.

Kerrigan and Meggie were going to spend the day together. Nate had to report to the police station for a few hours and Kerrigan wanted to keep Meggie with her. The two of them were playing house with Meggie's baby doll in Kerrigan's living room when Meggie's stomach growled.

"Someone sounds like she needs some lunch," Kerrigan said, tickling Meggie's little belly as she giggled in return.

"I thought we were going to wait for my daddy," Meggie said, sitting close to Kerrigan on the floor.

"We are, and he should be home soon, so let's take a walk over to his house and see what we can make for all of us to eat, okay?"

Meggie was dragging more toys out of her bedroom at Nate's house when Kerrigan looked in the refrigerator and searched inside of a few cabinets. She considered turkey sandwiches or grilled cheese as she stood in front of the counter and glanced down at the prescription pill bottle in Meggie's name. She remembered Nate telling her how Meggie was taking medication for her diabetes and must take one pill a day with food. She made a mental note to ask Nate if Meggie had to take one with her lunch. Out of curiosity, Kerrigan picked up the pill bottle and read it. She didn't recognize the generic form of medication, so she opened it and took out one of the pills and then she immediately took a closer look as she dumped a few more pills into the open palm of her hand.

She had seen this pill before. When she and Keith were trying to conceive, Kerrigan took one baby aspirin a day to try to increase the chances of a successful conception. Kerrigan learned then how it improves blood flow to the uterine lining and to the ovaries, producing healthier eggs, which results in healthier embryos. Kerrigan was positive she was staring at baby aspirin in her hand, but to be absolutely certain, she popped one into her mouth. It dissolved quickly on her tongue and left that familiar taste in her mouth.

Kerrigan checked on Meggie, playing in the middle of the living room floor and went back into the kitchen. She found a piece of scrap paper in a drawer and jotted down the name of the medication on the pill bottle. Glipizide. She planned to research it later, when she was alone.

Nate walked in the door before she could give this another thought, but Kerrigan was puzzled and wanted to get to the bottom of why Meggie's prescription medicine was anything but.

***

During lunch, Kerrigan watched Nate give Meggie one aspirin to take with her food. She kept her thoughts to herself. She couldn't say anything until she had more information.

When Kerrigan was waiting for Nate to finish reading a story to Meggie at bedtime, it seemed to have taken him awhile so she peeked her head inside of the bedroom since she no longer heard him reading aloud. That's when she saw them both, asleep. Kerrigan smiled to herself as she backed out of the doorway. She turned off the television and two lights in the living room and then she quietly left the house, locking the door behind her.

The first thing she did at her place was find her laptop. She had brought it along from Baltimore on her most recent trip when she packed up everything. Keith insisted she take the computer, and she knew why. Gail had every electronic under the sun. A desktop computer. A laptop. An iPad. An iPad mini. And always the latest in Apple's iPhone. She hoarded electronics.

Kerrigan sat down at the kitchen table after attaching and plugging in the power cord to her laptop. She immediately googled, Glipizide. She learned the medication is a generic form of sulfonylureas, given to both adults and children with Type 2 diabetes. Sulfonylurea medicines increase the amount of insulin produced by the pancreas to help control the blood sugar level. She understood all of that, but she knew the medication inside of the prescription bottle on Nate's counter with Meggie's name on it was not Glipizide. It, for sure, was baby aspirin. Now, she had to find out why.

She made her way back to Nate's house and when she turned the door handle on his front door, she found it locked. She was the one who locked it earlier. She sighed, realizing talking to Nate might just have to wait until tomorrow as she turned around to walk back home. And that's when Nate opened the door.

"I thought I heard an intruder," he teased. "Did you lock yourself out?"

"I locked your sleeping selves inside when I went back to my place for awhile," Kerrigan explained.

"Well I'm glad you came back," he said. "I'm a light sleeper, so you can wake me next time." Kerrigan walked past him and he snuggled up close behind her and guided her over the couch. He pulled her down on top of his lap and kissed her full on the mouth. He had not kissed her, and they had not shared any intimacy, since before her trip back to Baltimore. It felt comfortable being close to him again, but Kerrigan pulled away to talk.

"Slow down, big boy," she said laughing as she got off of his lap and sat down next to him.

"It's been too long..." Nate whined and Kerrigan shushed him by putting a finger up to his lips and he licked it.

"I was hoping we could talk," she said.

"About what?"

"The night Hallie died in the hospital," Kerrigan began, "and I saw Jenny there. I didn't know she's a nurse and I got to thinking, I don't even know what Bryn does for a living."

"She's a pharmacist," Nate replied, and Kerrigan's curiosity peaked. "She is?"

"Yeah, why the sudden interest in their careers?"

"Oh, no specific reason. I was just curious, I guess. Are they still together?" Kerrigan added.

"If Jenny had her way they would be, but Bryn is confused about them right now."

"Confused? So are they still living together?" Kerrigan inquired.

"I think so." Nate said.

"You haven't asked her?" Kerrigan was feeling annoyed.

"No, because I keep trying to avoid talking about her romantic life to keep her from making plays for me," Nate confessed.

"Has she come on to you?" Kerrigan had not forgotten seeing Bryn's car parked at the beach all night long the night she was called to the hospital to be with Hallie.

"Yes, she has tried to. I haven't responded, Kerrigan. I don't want her anymore, and she knows that and it just seems like lately she will try anything to get my attention."

"What do you mean by anything?" Kerrigan asked, thinking of Meggie.

"She cooks something for me almost every night, she comes by with Meggie and makes excuses how Meggie is feeling sad about her diabetes, not being able to eat candy, and having to take medicine. It's little excuses all of the time just to see me."

"If you realize this, why do you allow her to get away with it?" Kerrigan asked him.

"Because of Meggie. I will tolerate Bryn because she is Meggie's mother, but I will not become a family with her again." Nate appeared firm in his answer and Kerrigan believed him. She trusted him, she always had. It's Bryn she believed was the one to worry about and watch out for.

"So, where did she sleep that night when I was called to the hospital?" Kerrigan asked, watching Nate's face. "I saw her car parked out here at two in the morning."

"On the couch, where she passed out after drinking too much wine with dinner. I would not let her drive. She wanted to stay anyway so she never argued with me on that, but I did piss her off when I called Jenny to come and pick her up. Unfortunately, Jenny was on duty at the hospital so I didn't have any other choice but to allow her to stay overnight." The story made sense, and it also made Kerrigan dislike Bryn even more than she already had.

"So, she came on to you? Did she take off her clothes?" Kerrigan asked. "She's beautiful, Nate. Her body rocks something fierce compared to anyone, especially mine."

"We've been over this, Kerrigan," Nate said, leaning toward her. "I've already said you're it for me…and I want to take you as you are for the rest of my life."

"Take me?" Kerrigan asked as she instantly dropped the subject of Bryn. She had enough information, for now. She didn't need to press the issue tonight. She would begin to investigate further tomorrow. Right now, she only wanted Nate *to take her*.

She didn't feel like she was losing weight any longer or firming up her muscles, because she had gotten away from any form of exercise on the beach. She wanted to eat healthier and get into a routine of working out again, and she planned to. But, at the moment, she wasn't thinking about her lovies, the extra roll between under her breasts, her flabby stomach, or her full rear end and thick thighs. She felt curvy and beautiful when she was in Nate's arms because he made her feel that way. It made her crazy when he placed his thumbs under her chin and his other fingers along her jawbone as he pressed his lips to hers and intertwined his tongue with hers. It had been too long, and they wanted this again, so much.

They ended up in Nate's bed, still fully clothed. Behind the locked bedroom door, Nate kneeled on his bed as he slipped off Kerrigan's shorts and underwear, both at once again, and she removed her t-shirt and bra and threw both on the floor. By now, Nate had his shirt off and Kerrigan went for the zipper on his shorts. He knelt over her and she stripped him. He was a man of great size, everywhere, and Kerrigan could not resist taking him into her mouth. He came close to climaxing, but he didn't. It was Kerrigan's turn to be driven half out of her mind by him. Nate found his mouth between her legs and he never stopped until Kerrigan called out for *Jesus* and momentarily lay spent, naked, in his bed. He wasted no time plunging inside of her as the two of them became one again. Body and soul.

Chapter 21

She searched through the clothes hanging in MJ's closet. There had to be something in there that would fit her. MJ was as tall as Kerrigan and very up and down with her weight. Kerrigan had not seen MJ in almost two years, but she knew MJ's habit of keeping all of her clothes. Old styles. New styles. Fat clothes. Skinny clothes. Right now, Kerrigan hoped to find something from MJ's chunky era. And she did.

She pulled out a pale yellow sundress on a hanger. It was not as long as she would like for it to be, but Kerrigan slipped it over her head and actually loved the end result. The material didn't feel cheap and she could not see through it. The straps were wider than spaghetti straps and her cleavage was mostly covered. The dress ended about two inches above her knees and her now tan legs complimented her appearance today. She found a pair of straw-colored wedges on the floor in the back of MJ's closet. They wore the same size shoe in college, so Kerrigan knew those would fit. She looked at herself in the full-length mirror in the corner of the bedroom. She liked what she saw. Her hair was pulled up into a thick knot on top of her head and she felt girly. And even sexy. She considered keeping the dress on for Nate to see later, but right now it was Monday morning and he was at work, and Kerrigan was going to make a trip into town. To the pharmacy.

Kerrigan thought about what she would say when she got there, as she planned for Bryn to be working behind the counter. When she whipped her jeep into an open parking space directly in front of the pharmacy building, she saw Bryn's red sports car parked in the lot.

A bell on the door rang loudly when she entered. Kerrigan was greeted by a woman, probably in her mid-to-late fifties, working the check-out counter. She walked to the far end of the store with her eyes on the woman behind the pharmaceutical counter, with her back to her. Her very long, straight-as-a-poker, blonde hair looked shiny. Her white lab coat hung lower than the skirt she wore underneath it. Her legs were bare and very tan. She wore nude, high stilettos and Kerrigan wondered how her feet and legs could tolerate the stress of wearing those shoes all day long. Kerrigan stopped staring as Bryn turned around from placing a medicine order in one of the cubbies against the wall.

"Oh, hi," Bryn said, withholding speaking Kerrigan's name. She obviously did not want to get too personal. "Can I help you with something?" she asked, sizing up Kerrigan in her dress and wedges. Kerrigan's confidence did not waver. *This was not about who was more beautiful, who rocks the better body, or who had Nate's heart. This was about Meggie.*

"Hi Bryn. How are you?"

"Fine," she replied, coldy but not too rudely because she was *a professional* in her element right now. "What are you here for today?" Bryn would have remembered if she had seen an order come through for her. Kerrigan was not a typical first name.

Kerrigan smiled with her lips pressed tightly together, showing no teeth. "I need to pick up a refill of Glipizide for Meggie." Bryn's expression was a combination of surprise and irritation.

"I handle my daughter's medication refills," she said, with a serious frown on her face.

"Oh, I know you do, you're the pharmacist," Kerrigan tried to keep from smirking. She did not trust this woman. At all. "I'm just here to refill the prescription bottle you left at Nate's house, or remind you to bring more when Meggie stays with us again next weekend. *Us.* That word unnerved Bryn and she didn't hide that fact.

"I will bring more then," Bryn replied as another customer walked up and waited behind Kerrigan. "Is there anything else you need today, Kerrigan?" Bryn asked, stating her name, coldly, this time.

"No, thank you," Kerrigan replied. "I just need to pick up some baby aspirin before I leave." Bryn's face flushed and Kerrigan glared at her before she turned on the thick heels of her wedges and walked away. Kerrigan could feel Bryn's eyes on her as she found the shelf with baby aspirin, picked up a box and walked over to the cashier. She would need those baby aspirin to show Nate how the few pills left in the prescription bottle of medicine for his daughter are not what his ex-wife said they were.

***

"I think you should ask Bryn if you can go along to Meggie's next doctor's appointment," Kerrigan suggested to Nate while the two of them were standing in his kitchen, preparing to take vegetable seafood lasagna out of the oven for dinner.

"Why?" Nate asked. "She hasn't needed me to go along to any of her other appointments."

"Have you offered to go along? Kerrigan asked.

"Not really, but I would go if she asked me or needed me to," Nate said, sincerely.

"Nate, there is something you need to know and I hesitated to say anything until I knew for sure. I mean, I know I'm right about this and I'm not trying to cause trouble. I just want to get to the truth."

"What truth?" he asked. Kerrigan walked over the counter and opened Meggie's prescription medicine bottle. She dumped the three remaining pills onto the counter. Then she walked over to her handbag, which was hanging on the back of one of the kitchen chairs, and she took out the baby aspirin.

"I opened this pill bottle a few days ago, just curious about what type of medication Meggie needs and I discovered baby aspirin in here. I've taken those aspirin before, I tried one to be sure, and now I have a bottle of baby aspirin here. See for yourself." Kerrigan dumped the pills side by side.

Nate walked over there and studied both. "What the hell? This is crazy! So, Meggie does not need medicine for her diabetes?"

"I don't know," Kerrigan said, "but I think Bryn is up to something crazy…maybe a ploy to get your attention."

"She would never use Meggie like that!" Nate raised his voice. "She was just as distraught as I was when we first found out Meggie isn't healthy."

"I'm not saying she doesn't love her daughter, or that she isn't a good mother," Kerrigan defended herself. "I just find this weird and so was Bryn's reaction at the pharmacy today."

"What? You confronted her?" Nate seemed angry.

"I went in there to buy some baby aspirin and we chatted for a few minutes," Kerrigan said, wondering if this was going to end up being an argument between them.

"I'm so confused," Nate said. "Bryn is a pharmacist. She handles our daughter's medicine and now you're telling me there is no medicine."

"Nate, you can see for yourself!" Kerrigan said, feeling annoyed, as she pointed to the pills on the counter.

"I know I can," he replied looking at the aspirin again and shaking his head.

"Then find out what the hell this means. I'm not doing this to up the score between me and your ex-wife. I care about Meggie, I love her as my–" Kerrigan almost said *own*, but she stopped herself. *Dammit*, she missed Piper.

"I know you do," Nate said. "I'm sorry, I'm just tense about this. I trust Bryn."

"You trusted her to be faithful, too." Kerrigan responded. "You're a cop, Nate. Investigate this."

"I will forget my badge and tear her apart if she's been lying to me about something like this. It's Meggie for chrissakes. She's just a little girl. We had to tell her she is sick and needs special care with certain things, like what she eats."

"I'm just as upset about this as you are," Kerrigan said, walking toward him and wrapping her arms around his torso.

"Then be here with me when I call Bryn to get her ass over here, tonight," Nate replied.

***

When Nate opened the door of his beach house, Bryn was standing there alone. "Where's Meggie?" he asked as she stepped into his house and noticed Kerrigan standing behind the armchair.

"She is with Jenny. You sounded serious on the phone, so I didn't want Meggie to overhear anything crazy between us."

"Why do you say, crazy?" Nate asked her as she looked over at Kerrigan.

"Can we have a private conversation, please?" Bryn asked her ex-husband.

"Kerrigan stays," he responded, "because she is the reason I need some answers from you right now."

"Okay…" Bryn said as her voice trailed off and she appeared nervous to Kerrigan. Nate told Bryn to follow him and Kerrigan into the kitchen, and in there he showed her the pills on the counter.

"These pills that you said our daughter needs, the pill I make sure she gets when she's with me at lunchtime, are baby aspirin." Nate remained calm and Kerrigan stayed silent as Bryn immediately spoke.

"You did not handle Meggie's diagnosis very well and that worried me," Bryn began, as Nate frowned at her, but he remained patient and listened to her. "At one of Meggie's doctor's appointments I was told she will have to be on medicine within the next few months. I was just trying to prepare Meggie and you for when she does. Meggie is little and getting her into a routine of having to take medicine, probably for the rest of her life, is something I decided to do by using baby aspirin, at first." Kerrigan was floored. She did everything she could not to blurt out, *bullshit!*

"And you decided to lie about it?" Nate asked. "You should have at least told me what the hell you were doing. Are all of these baby aspirin safe for her?"

"I didn't want to stress you out even more," Bryn explained, appearing teary-eyed. "And yes, Meggie is fine taking one a day, everyone with diabetes should, to prevent heart risks."

"From here on, I want you to share everything with me about our daughter," Nate told Bryn, obviously feeling satisfied with her explanation. An explanation that Kerrigan found to be completely absurd. "And I want to go along to her doctor's appointments, every one of them."

"I want you to be included," Bryn said, smiling at him as if she scored. As if that was her goal all along. Getting Nate to spend more time with them. With her. And Kerrigan could have barfed. After a little more conversation, mostly regarding Meggie, took place between them in the kitchen, Bryn said she had to get back home.

When she left, Nate spoke first. "So, now we have that figured out. Bryn does that sometimes, she takes her professional knowledge and goes full speed ahead with things. I do not condone her making that decision without me and not telling me, but I can see how she wants to prepare Meggie to take medicine on a daily basis. Meggie hates medicine the way it is, you know for a cold or a fever or something." Kerrigan wanted to say *who does that? Really, who fucking lies about something as serious as medicine?* But, she remained silent and pretended to be in agreement.

Chapter 22

A week passed and the subject of Meggie's medication never came up again. Kerrigan was beginning to think she should just let it go, but it was Meggie who changed her mind.

The two of them were on the beach. Kerrigan was sitting in the sand as Meggie attempted to push her baby stroller through the viscous sand with her baby doll strapped inside of it. She was making circles around Kerrigan when Kerrigan teased her, "Your baby is going to get dizzy!" Kerrigan giggled, but Meggie's face grew serious before she spoke.

"Kerrigan, do you want a baby of your own?" The question was honest and completely innocent coming from a four year old, but it instantly hurt just to think of how she once had a baby of her own, for five short weeks, and may never be given that kind of gift again.

"Sure, I do," Kerrigan responded, "but right now I have you to love." Meggie's face lit up and Kerrigan wanted to keep focusing on her and what a gift she was in her life. She and Nate have been her saving grace. Hallie, too, but now Kerrigan had been forced to go on without her. She thought of Hallie day and night and even talked to her when she was alone. Kerrigan felt certain Hallie could hear her from heaven and she found comfort in knowing she could still count on her guidance.

"Are you going to make up stories, too? And keep secrets when you have a baby of your own?" Meggie asked as she sat down in the sand next to Kerrigan.

"I don't know what you mean," Kerrigan said to Meggie. "Why would I need to do that?"

"I'm not sure why," Meggie said, playing with the sand around the flip flops on her feet, "but my mommy says it's important for me to play along sometimes."

"Play along with what?" Kerrigan asked.

"I can't tell you because you don't like to keep secrets," Meggie said.

"I never said I don't like to, it just depends on why we're keeping secrets. Like if it's a birthday surprise for someone and we don't want that person to know about their presents or their party, then it's okay to keep a secret. Meggie, there are good secrets and then there are bad secrets. Please tell me what you are talking about," Kerrigan said, feeling impatient and worried at the same time.

"I have to say I go to the doctor and I have to say I can't eat candy and I have to take a vitamin when I eat my lunch." Meggie's response confused Kerrigan.

"Are you saying that you really don't go to the doctor with your mommy?"

"I went to the doctor when I had a bad cough and a fever right before I had a birthday, when I was still three," Meggie said.

"Oh…" Kerrigan responded. "So do you still eat candy?"

"Only when I'm at my house where I live with my mommy and Jenny," she confessed.

"But not when you're with daddy?" Kerrigan asked.

"No, but when I'm at daddy's house I have to take a vitamin." Meggie seemed happy to tell Kerrigan *her secret*, and Kerrigan was desperately trying to hide her shocked feelings. Bryn was up to something strange and this time Kerrigan was not going to let her talk her way out of it, or get away with it.

***

Kerrigan never had a chance to talk to Nate about her suspicions because when he returned from his run on the beach while she played in the sand with Meggie, he received a call to report to the police station. On his way out, he reminded Kerrigan of Bryn coming by to pick up Meggie tonight. *Great,* she thought to herself. *I'm sure she will be thrilled to see me alone with her daughter.*

It wasn't Bryn who came by though, it was Jenny. Meggie seemed happy to see her and obeyed her when Jenny told her to gather all of her things, especially her favorite baby doll that she hauled everywhere. While Meggie was in her bedroom at Nate's house, Jenny and Kerrigan were alone.

"So where's Bryn tonight?" Kerrigan asked, trying to make conversation but realizing she appeared nosy.

"Working late," Jenny responded as Kerrigan noticed how fit she looked wearing her hospital scrubs. She was more muscular than Bryn, and not as striking. Her short, cropped hair and the definition in her arms and legs made her look too manly, Kerrigan thought, but realized that was the look Jenny was after.

"So is Nate," Kerrigan said. "Should we be worried they are together?" Kerrigan joked, but then she wondered if Jenny truly trusted Bryn anymore.

"Bryn and I are really trying to make our relationship work," Jenny said, sounding defensive and obviously feeling insecure about their relationship.

It seemed obvious to Kerrigan how this woman was scared to death of losing her girlfriend. "Does Bryn want your relationship to work?" Kerrigan asked, feeling bold and most definitely prying where she had no right to.

"I don't know what you want me to say, but anything I do say is going to push Bryn away from me if she finds out you and I were even discussing her. Just please keep this between us." Jenny seemed uneasy. "She loves me," Jenny continued, still on the defense. "She just feels confused lately, ever since you came into Nate's life. Honestly, and she would ream me for saying this," Jenny paused, "she does not want him back. She just cannot handle you having him."

Kerrigan tried not to look as offended as she felt. "Because I'm not good enough? Pretty enough? Fit enough?" she asked, quickly reminding herself that Nate loves her for who she is. Inside and out.

"No," Jenny said, appearing sincere. "Because you're the first woman in Nate's life since she left him. I don't think she expected to react as she has." Kerrigan wanted to say. *How? Crazy? Because it is crazy to think Bryn could have fabricated the entire diabetes story at Meggie's expense. What an awful, sickening way to get Nate's attention.*

"Why are you okay with this?" Kerrigan asked her. "You must see how she goes out of her way to spend more time with Nate, and she has come on to him. She says she wants him back and she wants to be a family with him and then she turns around and crawls into bed with you when she gets home. That's not fair to you, Jenny," Kerrigan said, actually sounding as if she cared about her feelings.

"It's just a phase," Jenny said. "I've known Bryn all of my life. She and I cannot survive without each other."

"Then I hope the two of you find your happily ever after together," Kerrigan said, and she was being sincere. If two people love each other, they should be together. That is how Kerrigan felt about being with Nate. And she also felt like Bryn had been a dark cloud hanging over them. She didn't like her, and she didn't trust her.

As the evening hours passed, Kerrigan continued to think about Bryn and she was still dwelling when she was lying in bed at her beach house at quarter after one in the morning.

***

"Something is off," Kerrigan said to Nate the following day.

"With us?" he asked her as she instantly had his attention. He was still wearing his work clothes, jeans and a white polo shirt, and he had stepped up onto her deck, where she lounged in the sun.

"No," she smiled at him. "With your ex."

Nate rolled his eyes. "Now what did she do? Did you two get into it when she picked up Meggie last night? A catfight in my living room?" Nate was not taking any of this seriously and Kerrigan wondered if she too should start blowing off anything regarding Bryn. This was not just about Bryn though. This was about Meggie.

"She didn't come by, Jenny did," Kerrigan said, "and Jenny and I had a little chat about how solid her relationship is with Bryn. She told me that Bryn does not want you back, she just does not want me with you."

"I think she was jealous, but she has begun to move past that," Nate defended her. "It doesn't matter how she feels. You need to be confident in how I feel about you."

"I am," Kerrigan said.

"But?" Nate asked.

"I've lost a lot in my life. I trusted my best friend would always be there. I trusted my husband loved me and only me. And I trusted that God had finally answered my prayers and made me a mother for life, not for five weeks." As Kerrigan spoke, she left out how she trusted her foster parents loved her, despite the fact that she never felt wanted by them. And she also refrained from mentioning Hallie. Missing her was still too raw. As Nate listened, he felt sympathetic.

"I know you have been through hell with the people you loved, more than anyone should have to," he said, "but I'm not them – and neither is Bryn. She is not like your superficial friend, Gail. She's a good person and a good mother. Can we just move on with our lives and not worry about everyone else?" Kerrigan listened to Nate with an open mind, and then she decided now was not the time to accuse Bryn of lying about Meggie's health and playing games to win Nate's attention. If Bryn was lying, the truth would come out. It always does.

So Kerrigan took Nate's words to heart, and she promised herself to try to let go of the hurt from her past, and concentrate on enjoying the present and moving forward with her life.

Chapter 23

The following two weeks were busy for Kerrigan. Hallie's lawyer had contacted her to finalize the will. She received the official documents stating how she now owned all three of the beach houses, and all of Hallie's assets. Kerrigan also received a check in her name for nine hundred and eighty-five thousand dollars. It didn't seem real how everything Hallie owned was now hers, but it became clearer to Kerrigan as she began to move some of her things out of MJ's beach house and into Hallie's. It was already August, but Kerrigan remained living at MJ's beach house since she was not expected to return for another four weeks.

The first time Kerrigan walked back into Hallie's house, it was difficult. She had not gone back in there after Hallie died. Keeping her house closed and locked up mirrored how Kerrigan never wanted to go back into Piper's nursery after she lost her. She opened the window blinds when she entered the living room. Hallie always loved letting the sun shine in and being able to see the view outside. Kerrigan looked around the quiet room and all of the pictures were staring back at her. She didn't know how much of the furniture in Hallie's place she would eventually swap out for her own, which was still in storage in Baltimore, but one thing she knew for certain was those photographs would remain. At least the ones with Hallie in them. She never wanted to forget her. She still wanted to see her face every day.

***

Kerrigan had spent all day going back and forth between the two houses. She sat down on the couch at MJ's and tipped back a glass of wine. Nate was working late and she planned to continue going through some more of Hallie's things over at her place, after she took a short break and drank her wine.

Her cell phone, placed on the coffee table next to where she had her bare feet propped up, rang and Kerrigan was surprised to see Keith calling her. Their contact had ceased for more than a month. She let her phone ring another time before she answered.

"Kerrie, hi," It was Keith's familiar voice on the other end. "I hope all is well."

"I am doing well," she said. "How are you, Keith?"

"Great, and I have some good news for you!" he stated, sounding happy and as if he instantly wanted to get to the point of his call. "The house sold. I ended up dickering a bit and got one hundred and five for it."

"That's good," Kerrigan said, realizing she had forgotten about the house needing to sell. She knew their debt, so she had not been expecting any money from the sale. Kerrigan felt extreme gratitude to Hallie for not having to worry about any immediate income now. She intended to get a job at summer's end, once MJ returned, and she made the move from her place to Hallie's.

"Yeah, it is," Keith agreed. "I was able to pay off our loan, and our credit card debt. I only wish I could have made a little money and sent you some, for you to get on your feet there in Orange Beach."

"Thank you, but I wasn't counting on any," Kerrigan said, thinking about how she needed to find a bank now for the money she received from Hallie. All of this felt surreal to her. She came to Orange Beach only planning to stay for the summer, and now she was making a life there and for the first time in her adult life, she did not have to worry about her next paycheck. She felt grateful, but she knew it would continue to feel strange for awhile.

"Are you working anywhere yet?" Keith asked.

"Not yet," Kerrigan responded. "I'm going to wait until the end of summer to look for a job."

"Okay," Keith replied.

"How are things with you…and Gail?" She didn't want to ask, but she did anyway.

"We're good, Kerrie…" he said, and paused, before he carefully added, "We've heard the baby's heartbeat a few times." There it was again. The painful truth. Gail has Keith's baby, healthy and growing, inside of her. Kerrigan's silence on the phone prompted Keith to speak again. "I'm sorry if I'm being insensitive."

"It's okay," Kerrigan tried to reassure him. "Won't be long and you can find out what you're having." Kerrigan didn't want to know and she certainly didn't want to keep talking to Keith about this, but she suffered through it.

"Yeah," he said softly on his end.

"There is something I would like to ask you to do for me, if you will," Kerrigan said, changing the subject and trying to make this conversation less awkward between them.

"Sure, name it," Keith offered.

"Send me the furniture and things that you have in storage for me, please."

"Already? What about a place to stay? I thought you wanted to wait until you moved out of MJ's and got settled somewhere." Keith wondered if she was going to pay for storage there.

"I have a place to stay already," Kerrigan answered. "I'm going to be living on the beach in the house next to MJ's. It became available." Kerrigan felt sad, thinking how it became available. But, she also felt incredible gratitude for Hallie again. For being in her life. And for continuing to take care of her.

"That's wonderful," Keith said, genuinely feeling happy for her, but he worried she may be too lonely there. He still felt guilty for moving on so quickly, assuming Kerrigan had not.

"Yes, it is. I love it here. I could see myself making a life here." *With Nate. And Meggie.*

"I'm glad," Keith said. "Keep me updated on what's going on with you." Kerrigan wanted to say, *you do the same,* but she didn't because she couldn't bear to hear about Gail and their baby. All she responded was, *okay,* and their conversation ended shortly after she gave Keith the address to the beach house. She planned to decide how to furnish Hallie's house with some of her own furniture, too.

***

Everything seemed to be falling into place in her life again, and Kerrigan was well aware of what it meant to count her blessings as she picked up her pace while walking along the beach. Mornings were especially peaceful out there, and she made sure she got up early to relish in that every day. She was beginning to like her body, and she did not remember a time in her life when she did. She was not thin or fabulously fit, but she felt tighter in places and in better shape than she had been in years. M.J. did not have a scale in her house, so Kerrigan was uncertain of how much weight she had lost, but when her elastic-wasted athletic shorts became loose fitting, she felt thrilled to think she may have gone down a size, or two. And, she was excited to think about being able to use a little of her money, now in the bank, to start a new wardrobe. *Change is good*, Kerrigan thought, as she neared the end of her walk, sighting her deck and beach house in the distance. All three of those houses were hers. She smiled to herself, remembering when Nate brought up how he owes her rent each month now, and she told him it would feel strange taking money from him because they share so much of their lives. He insisted on paying her, and she gave in. She had already decided that MJ would not owe her any rent for at least four months once she returned, because she too had been generous to Kerrigan by allowing her to live in her home all summer long.

MJ, however, did not return to her beach house. She had texted Kerrigan in late August and told her to stay as long as she wanted. She was uncertain when she would return home. She then added, *tell Hallie I will owe her a few months of back pay, with interest*. Her words tugged at Kerrigan's heart strings. She wished she could tell Hallie.

***

The sun was beginning to set as Nate and Kerrigan sat on the lounge chairs on her deck. Kerrigan was sipping a Diet Coke and Nate didn't want anything, but had taken a long drink of hers while they sat there talking.

The late summer air was cooler than it had been all season long and Kerrigan liked the feel of the season beginning to change. She felt at peace with her life and she relished in this new beginning she was embarking on.

A few weeks ago, Nate had helped her move into Hallie's beach house after the furniture arrived from Baltimore. She kept Hallie's recliner, but moved her own couch in. She donated an armchair of Hallie's and her bed to Goodwill. And then she and Nate made a trip to a local furniture store to pick out a new bed. The owner of the furniture store wore a contagious smile, he said his name was Marty, and he laughed out loud when Kerrigan said she was looking for a sleigh bed. And then Marty found a catalog for her, and she ordered a queen-sized sleigh bed from him. She remembered what she thought the first time she saw MJ had a sleigh bed in her beach house. *It looked like something that belonged inside of a log cabin, not a beach house. That is just like MJ. If you like something, who cares if it doesn't go? Think outside of the box. Be different. To hell with what should or shouldn't be.* Kerrigan wished then she could develop a mindset like that. And now, four months later, she knew she had.

She still spent time inside of MJ's place, and used her deck for the comfortable lounge chairs which they were sitting on now, but her home had become the middle house on the beach. "What are you thinking about?" Nate asked her, reaching out to touch her hand as they began to lose daylight.

"My life…and how much has fallen into place just by being here," Kerrigan said, as she sighed and then smiled at him.

"It has, hasn't it?" he said. "From the moment you arrived, my life changed. Something inside of me came alive again, and I found a reason to feel complete."

"You're just saying that because you wanna get into my new sleigh bed, which arrived today," Kerrigan teased him and he laughed at her.

"That too," he replied, never having loved her more than he did at this moment. And this perfect moment, this beautiful evening could not be wasted. Nate reached into the pocket of his baggy navy blue gym shorts as Kerrigan watched him move down onto the surface of the deck, onto one knee.

"I did this once before, unofficially," he said, with his eyes twinkling, "and now it's time to do it, officially." Kerrigan sat upright in her chair, with wide eyes that immediately felt teary. "You, Kerrigan Fred Ross, make my heart happy," he winked and she giggled at him. "I want to love you for the rest of my life, if you will have me as yours. Marry me…"

By now, Kerrigan tasted the tears trickling steadily down both of her cheeks. "You saved me, do you know that?

You saved me from my sadness. You taught me how to seize the moment and savor it for all it's worth. I love you, Nate. I love you with everything I have."

"I love you more," he said. "So, is that a yes?"

"It's a yes!" she said, ending up on both of her knees in front of him as he slipped the one and a half carat diamond, set on a wide gold band, on her finger. And, then they kissed. Very soon after they became an engaged couple, they made their way over to the middle beach house to christen that new sleigh bed.

Chapter 24

In early spring, a simple white sundress, which reached her ankles when she slipped it on at the department store, was spread out across the duvet on Kerrigan's bed. It was her wedding dress and her and Nate's wedding day was here.

They planned to exchange their vows in front of a minister and Meggie. From this day forward, they would begin their life together and Kerrigan was smiling to herself in front of the mirror as she thought how excited Nate was to marry her. For months, he had talked about her becoming his wife and today his dream, and hers, would become a reality.

Nate had not seen her this morning, because he promised to wait and first set eyes on her when she walked down her deck, and onto the sand, to join him for their vows. Meggie was with Nate as Kerrigan stood in her bedroom, wearing only her bra and underwear before she got dressed. Her long, dark curls were in an updo today, and her makeup looked flawless. She rarely wore any, so looking at her own reflection made Kerrigan stare a little longer. She not only felt beautiful, she believed she looked beautiful.

Her fascination with her own appearance on her wedding day was instantly interrupted by her cell phone ringing over on the dresser top. Kerrigan walked over to it, assuming it was Nate wondering if she was ready, and then she saw it was Keith. She had not spoken to him since she sent him a courtesy text six months ago when her furniture arrived. It was best if he did not know she was getting married today. And it was best she did not know if his baby had been born yet. Kerrigan pondered if she should even answer his call right now. His timing was not the best.

But, she answered anyway. "Hi Keith…I'm hoping your call isn't urgent because I'm about to walk out the door." *And down the aisle.*

Kerrigan could hear him sobbing on the opposite end of the phone. She felt pangs of panic and her memory flashed back too quickly to witnessing him grieve for their baby. She had never seen him cry in all the years they had been together, until then. And she would never forget the pain of watching a grown man fall to pieces.

"Keith! What is wrong?" Kerrigan tried to get him to stop crying and talk to her, but it felt like endless minutes before he attempted to speak and she managed to make out his words.

"Gail… died…while… giving… birth." Keith broke into sobs again, and Kerrigan froze. She never wanted to see her best friend again, but she never, ever, would have wished her any harm. She could not be dead. Not a tough cookie like her. Not a woman who got what she wanted at any and all costs. Not the eight-year-old little girl who befriended her and felt like her sister for most of her life. Not the friend she loved and lost and tucked away somewhere deep inside of her heart. *This could not be true!*

"Oh my God, Keith! No, no, no. Please no." Kerrigan tried to calm herself down as she spoke, because Keith sounded completely out of control. "Tell me what happened."

"The amniotic fluid got into her bloodstream when she was in labor," Keith began to explain, while choking on his sobs. "She was conscious and she knew…she knew she had to make a choice. The doctor was very clear about only one of them surviving this…" Keith broke down again and Kerrigan felt as if she was going to pass out. She sat down on the end of her bed, wrinkling her wedding dress. She knew what had happened. It's rare, but she had heard of it before. An amniotic fluid embolism causes catastrophic shutdown of all the organs. Once fluid enters the mother's bloodstream, respiratory failure occurs. Many times, it

Heartless

happens and it's too late. In Gail's case, the signs were evident – and a choice had to be made.

Kerrigan had momentarily forgotten about the baby's life. She had been putting that baby out of her mind for several months. She didn't want to know about it. "Are you telling me, Gail gave her life to save her baby?" It was unbelievable. The most selfish person Kerrigan had ever known was responsible for the most selfless act ever.

"She said she could not bear to see me lose another baby…she said she could not be the one to take her from me. She chose to die in order for my daughter to live." Keith was beside himself and the word *daughter* was ringing in Kerrigan's ears. He had another daughter. Another chance. Another gift. A new life to hold in his arms, thanks to Gail Boyd.

"I can't believe this," Kerrigan spoke, softly. "I have loved Gail for so many reasons, but I ended up hating her for the person she could be sometimes. But, now, knowing she is gone and knowing what she gave up…makes me so sad and so damn proud of her at the same time." Kerrigan was not crying, but her heart ached for this loss. Another loss.

***

Kerrigan was shaking when she ended that call with Keith. She was still wearing only her lacy white bra and matching underwear when she picked up her dress off of the bed and slipped into it. How quickly one of the happiest days of her life had turned sad. She remained barefoot, because she had not planned to wear any shoes in the sand when she got married. She chose tan linen pants and a long-sleeved white dress shirt for Nate to wear, also with no shoes, and that's what he was wearing when Kerrigan walked next door and entered his house. She was twenty minutes early, the minister had not even arrived yet, and she was not supposed to be there. She looked beautiful to him at first glance, but he covered his eyes immediately and spoke. "I'm not supposed to see you, yet!" he pretended to be afraid to jinx their happy life together as Kerrigan asked him to stop. "I need to talk to you, Nate. It's important."

Nate removed his hands from his eyes and looked at her. He really looked at her this time and he saw pain in her eyes. It's been awhile, but it was familiar for him to see her hurting and he was scared of what she was about to say to him.

"Keith called me, just now," she began to explain. "His baby was born this morning. There was a serious complication during the labor…and Gail died." Kerrigan still felt too shocked to feel, to really feel the emotion and the finality of this. Maybe she was afraid to. Maybe she was just sick and tired of death and grieving and the ongoing presence of it in her life.

"What?" Nate walked over to her and took both of her hands in his. "That is just crazy. I'm sorry, I don't know what else to say. A mother dying, leaving her baby behind, is awful."

"Yes, it is awful, but she was well aware of what she was doing. She wanted her baby to live. She chose her daughter's life over her own." Kerrigan felt pride surface in her heart again. "She wanted Keith to be a dad."

"I'm sure he's heartbroken, and despite everything you have to feel sorry for the guy. Raising a child, a baby, alone, is not easy," Nate sympathized.

"Gail didn't want Keith to raise her alone," Kerrigan said, feeling her eyes widen and still not being able to completely comprehend her former friend's final wish. "She told Keith to bring me back into his life, to be a mother to their baby girl."

Nate backed up from Kerrigan. "You can't be serious? She had a death wish and now he wants you back? He hurt you, he chose your best friend over you when you needed him the most! Don't you see he's in need of a mother for his baby and now you're good enough?" Nate felt panic emerge inside of him. *Kerrigan could not possibly be considering this. He's a father and he knew how that felt. A parent would sacrifice anything for a child. But this, this was just too much. That baby girl could not replace the baby girl Kerrigan lost. Life did not work that way. Their life together is supposed to begin today. Not fall apart.*

She just stared at him. She understood his fear right now. She felt it, too. She suddenly, and once again, had no idea what she was supposed to do with her life. Up until a matter of minutes ago, she was sure. She was certain of the path she was about to embark on. She loved Nate, and his little girl with all of her heart. Her saving graces. She wasn't sure she had enough of anything inside of her to give them up. To give up loving them and being loved by them. But, then, there was this chance, this opportunity which came out of nowhere, for her to be a mother again. A mother to a baby Gail left behind. *How can she turn her back on a baby? This could be her only chance.*

"This isn't about Keith," she said, wanting to clarify that to Nate. "This is about a baby."

"Kerrigan, please, don't let what happened to your baby make this decision, this life-changing decision, for you. We can try to have our own. It could happen."

"I want that so much," Kerrigan said to him, "but there is no guarantee I can conceive again."

"There are no guarantees in life!" Nate raised his voice. "You, of all people, know that. Don't throw us away."

"I can't marry you," Kerrigan said aloud, but her voice was barely a whisper.

"No!" Nate yelled at her and Kerrigan could see Meggie hovering in the doorway of her bedroom. She heard all of it, their entire conversation. Kerrigan didn't want to break her heart, too. Nate's was already shattering and her own heart was completely crumbling as she watched him.

Kerrigan walked quickly over to the doorway and knelt down in front of Meggie. The freckles on her face were wet with tears and Kerrigan attempted to wipe them away with her own fingers. "Don't cry," Kerrigan said, feeling her own eyes welling up. And Meggie responded, "Don't leave us."

Kerrigan pulled that little girl into her arms and held her. She saw Nate sit down on the couch, wearing his tan linen pants and the sleeves on his white long-sleeved dress shirt were now rolled up to his elbows as she watched him put his face into his hands. Kerrigan stood up and guided Meggie into her bedroom and she closed the door behind them. The two sat down on Meggie's twin bed before Kerrigan spoke. "I don't want to leave you or your daddy, please believe that," Kerrigan told her. "I just can't marry your daddy today. A baby was born and her mommy died, and I feel like she needs me right now."

"I don't think that baby needs you as much as my daddy does," Meggie's words were breaking Kerrigan's heart.

"I need your daddy, too, and you," Kerrigan said.

"Then why do you have to leave us? I don't understand." Meggie's words forced Kerrigan to stop. "I don't understand either, Meggie. I just know I need to figure out a few things before I make any important decisions, like getting married."

"You should go tell my daddy that," Meggie said. "I'll wait here, in my room." Kerrigan pulled her close again, and whispered in her ear, "I will. I love you, sweet girl."

Kerrigan found Nate still sitting on the couch. "The minister showed...I told him there isn't going to be a wedding. Is that what you really want, Kerrigan?" Nate's eyes were red and teary, and Kerrigan felt terrible knowing how much she had hurt him.

"No. Of course it's not what I want," she answered, going over to sit beside him. "I need some time to figure this out. I don't know what I'm supposed to do."

"I get how this baby has stopped you in your tracks," Nate began, "I really do understand how your personal loss has you feeling drawn to this baby who does not have a mother, whose mother happened to mean the world to you at one time. What I don't understand is how you can possibly think about going back to Keith. You were not wholeheartedly happy with him, you told me so yourself."

"I've never loved a man the way that I love you, and I never will again," Kerrigan said, feeling torn between Nate and a newborn baby.

"Then don't go."

Chapter 25

Kerrigan was lying in her sleigh bed, tossing and turning. "I asked you to help me!" she cried out into the dark room. "Come on, Hallie. You said I could count on your guidance for the rest of my life! Well, where the hell are you now?"

She had a flight booked to go back to Baltimore in the morning. This time, she would fly. She was no longer concerned about not having the money to spare for a ticket, and she knew driving would take too long. Getting to the hospital to help Keith sort this out was something she believed she needed to do.

She must have finally dozed off as she heard it begin to rain outside. It only felt as if she had closed her eyes for a moment when lightening lit up her bedroom. When the room went dark again, she saw something in the doorway. A figure, something white. She was startled as she sat upright in her bed. It was Hallie, her snow-white hair, wearing an all-white muu-muu. Suddenly, any fear she felt had diminished. "You came," Kerrigan said.

"You didn't leave me much choice," Hallie spoke, and Kerrigan tried to move out of her bed and run to her, but her efforts failed so she sat still, hoping for this time with Hallie to go on forever. "It's time to get your head out of your ass, honey," Hallie said, and Kerrigan smiled. Not quite angel dialogue, but this wasn't just any angel, this was Hallie. "You know what you have to do. You know where you are needed. Remember what I said to you about my girls. Remember if I could have been heard, my whole life would have been different."

Kerrigan woke up with a start. The room was completely dark again and she could still hear the rain outside. Hallie was there. She may have come to her in the form of a dream, but she was there. Kerrigan remembered how she looked, so angelic and yet so Hallie. And Kerrigan also remembered every single word she had said. But, she was confused and frustrated by what she said. "No! I don't remember any one specific thing you said about your girls. You had so many stories! How am I supposed to know what you mean?" Kerrigan was yelling into the darkness as thunder cracked loudly in the sky. She knew that was Hallie's doing, and she felt annoyed as well as puzzled.

Morning came a few short hours later, and it was still raining. Kerrigan hurried to pack a full suitcase for her trip. She was tired of thinking about what she should or should not do, so she just packed and left, planning to be at the airport in less than a half an hour. Her flight was in one hour.

The rain was down pouring as Kerrigan stepped onto the deck without an umbrella. She clinched tightly to her suitcase and ran to her jeep. One turn of the key in the ignition and she got nothing. Kerrigan did not know a whole lot about cars, but she was experienced enough to know when you get nothing, you have a dead battery. "Fucking jeep!" she spoke aloud. She was already wet and she was about to get soaked as she ran back toward the beach and up to Nate's door, and the entire time it seemed like the rain inconveniently came down harder on her. Nate answered after she knocked a second time, and much harder. By now, she was soaked to the skin. So much for the pretty powder blue pirate blouse with three-quarter-length sleeves she was wearing with a pair of dark-washed jeans, which now fit, and wedges. Her shirt felt like soaked tissue paper, clinging to her wet skin.

Nate just looked at her for a moment before he quickly pulled her inside and shut the door. She left her suitcase in the jeep, so he had no idea she was leaving for the airport. She planned to call him later, after she landed. It would just be easier that way. "What are you doing out in this rain?" he asked her.

"Trying to leave, but my jeep's battery is dead," she explained. "Nate, I know I have no right to ask you this, but can you give me a ride to the airport?"

"No," he replied. "Take it as a sign."

From Hallie? She wondered if maybe it was. "I don't know how to read those signs," she said, feeling like Hallie's appearance to her last night was useless. *If she had something to tell me, just fucking tell me!*

"I don't have much time…I am going to miss my flight if you don't drive me." Kerrigan thought she saw a smirk on Nate's face.

"I told you, I'm not going to help you." He was serious, and Kerrigan was angry at him.

"Fine! I will call a cab!" Kerrigan fumbled through her handbag, looking for her cell phone. Thank God she had grabbed her handbag from inside the jeep before she ran out in the rain. Otherwise, she would be running out in the damn rain again. She called for a taxi and waited in front of Nate's window.

"You know, I can see right through that wet shirt," he said to her and Kerrigan turned around, feeling pissed.

"What? Great, I'm trying to get the hell out of here quickly in the first rain storm we've had all summer on this drought of a beach and you're telling me you can see my tits!"

Nate tried not to laugh at her. She looked both adorable and sexy to him at this moment. "What changed?" Kerrigan asked him. "You seem okay now. Do you want me to go?"

"I think you're the only one who has to *want* to go," Nate said. "I just feel better about this whole mess since I prayed about it last night."

"You pray?" Kerrigan had no idea if he prayed or not. They have never talked about it.

"Well, I talked to Hallie, which is sort of the same thing since she's...up there."

"So you saw her?" Kerrigan was intrigued to think they may have shared a similar experience last night.

"No, that would be weird and it would freak me out," Nate said. "I just talked to her, and asked for her help with you."

"And she helped you?" Kerrigan felt irked with Hallie again. Why couldn't she help her? They were interrupted by Kerrigan's cell phone ringing in her handbag, which hung on her shoulder. She reached for it and answered. The call lasted less than twenty seconds.

"The roads are flooded. No through traffic to the beach. The taxi won't be coming for me." Kerrigan sighed and dropped her handbag onto the floor at her feet. Her shoulders were slumped and she was shivering from being wet. Nate walked over to her and pulled her into his arms.

"Do not ask me again to take you to that damn airport, because I can't do it."

"I know! The roads are flooded," she said sarcastically as she pulled out of his arms.

"That is not what I mean," he continued. "I would paddle you in a goddamn boat if there was somewhere you needed to be. Kerrigan, I'm not all that special. I live a pretty simple life. All I want to do is work and come home to a family I love, and who loves me. That is all I've ever wanted. I may not be the most exciting man out there, but I am who I am. I have a little girl who lights up my world and I have a woman who makes me feel like my heart will burst if I love her any more than I already do."

Kerrigan did not take her eyes off of him. How could she? Here, stood a man who came into her life and filled it. He filled the gaps and eased her pain. By loving her.

"I panicked. I thought I had to seize the chance to be with that baby," she admitted. "What happened to me, losing Piper, has scarred me. I'm so terrified I won't have a baby, ever. But, now I see what I've done. I've let my fears own me...and I almost lost you – and Meggie – by doing so."

"We are still here," Nate said, taking her into his arms again. She held onto him tightly. For dear life. He is her life now. And she never again wanted to come this close to letting him go.

***

Kerrigan noticed the rain had stopped and the sun was beginning to peer through the dark clouds. As she walked into her beach house alone, she spotted her favorite picture of Hallie, the one of her looking sandwiched in the middle of her three daughters. Their arms were all around each other and their faces, their cheeks were so close together. Not even air could pass through. Their connection so solid. Untouchable. But, not really. The day those girls boarded that plane, everything changed. Ended. Lost. If only they hadn't gotten on that plane.

There it was. This was Kerrigan's *aha* moment. The picture on the coffee table had been turned, now facing the door. Kerrigan had it turned the other way so she could see it from the couch. She now remembered Hallie holding that picture against her chest as she spoke about the day her girls were killed. *"I didn't have a good feeling about it, but I kept my fears to myself. I was so excited to be able to see my girls. What I should have said is...Don't get on that plane. Drive instead. Or, stay put and I will come to you. Just please don't get on that plane!"*

Kerrigan stood there, staring at the photograph. "I didn't, Hallie," she said aloud as she smiled. The pouring down rain. The dead battery in her jeep. The flooded road leading to the beach. Hallie pulled out all stops to keep her there. Where she belonged.

Chapter 26

One day later, as the plane lifted off the ground, Kerrigan thought back to her phone conversation with Keith. He was beyond upset when she told him she would only be coming back to Baltimore for the funeral. She was not moving back. She was not going to help him raise his baby, Gail's baby. It would not be right for her to miss Gail's memorial service. She, of all people, shared the most memories with her. She had to be there, she had to say goodbye, but she was not going to raise Gail's baby as her own. Kerrigan knew how consumed with grief Keith was, so she excused his anger toward her on the phone.

She could still hear his hateful words. *"How could you not want to do this with me? God, Kerrigan, have a heart. What's happened to you in Orange Beach? You're not the same person anymore. You're letting us all down – me, the baby, and Gail. It was her final wish for chrissakes!"*

She wanted to tell him how he was right. She was not the same person who left Baltimore and ended up in Orange Beach a year ago. It had already been one year since her world exploded, and during that time she somehow managed to pick up the pieces. She didn't do it alone though. And during their phone conversation, she told Keith how she was getting married again. His silence compelled her to think he understood now. He had to realize her new life was most important to her now. It's the way life rolls. It's called, moving on.

As Kerrigan was deep in her thoughts, staring out of the airplane window, Nate reached for her hand from the seat beside her. "You okay?"

"I'm fine," she said, intertwining her fingers with his. "Thank you for coming with me. I don't think I could do this alone."

***

When their flight landed, there wasn't much time before the memorial service would begin. Kerrigan and Nate hurried through the airport, each holding a carry-on bag in their hand, and Nate immediately hailed a taxi once they were outside. They were already dressed for the service, knowing there would be no time to check into a hotel and change clothes. Kerrigan was wearing a long, sleeveless, straight black dress with a scoop neckline. The dress ended at her ankles and she wore black open-toe heels. Despite the fact that she was going to a funeral, Kerrigan looked radiant. Her suntan, her weight loss, and having Nate by her side had all played a huge factor in Kerrigan feeling and looking beautiful. She was quiet on the ride to the funeral home as she picked a piece of lint off of Nate's pant leg. He wore black dress pants, black patent tie-shoes, and a long-sleeved white dress shirt. He asked her again if he should put on a tie, because he brought one along just in case. "However you're comfortable," she answered him. He reached into his bag at his feet in the taxi and unzipped it. He looked at the gray and black checkered tie, which he had neatly folded and had readily accessible at the top of his bag, but he decided against wearing it. "I think I'll skip it."

"Are you nervous about going in?" Kerrigan asked him as the taxi sped through the streets of downtown Baltimore.

"No, not at all," he said. "I just know this isn't going to be easy for you."

When the taxi pulled up under the extensive overhang at the funeral home, Kerrigan got out of the backseat first, and Nate followed her. "Where should we put our bags?" Kerrigan asked him as Nate paid the driver. "I will ask the funeral director if we can put them in a closet or back room. I'm sure this isn't the first time some out-of-towners have arrived straight from the airport with luggage." Kerrigan didn't feel like an out-of-towner. Baltimore was her home for most of her life. And those people inside of this funeral home once were her family.

Nate caught the attention of an older man, wearing a gray three-piece suit as they entered the building. He immediately followed that man around the corner to a room which looked like an office from where Kerrigan stood. As she waited, she turned to the side and saw a short line had formed from the casket to the podium where a guest book had been placed. *Why would you want a guest book at a funeral home?* Kerrigan never understood that. *Do family members really go back and read those names? Does it really matter who took the time to write down their name?* Kerrigan was trying to think of anything and everything to keep her mind off of who laid lifeless in that casket, pushed up against the wall.

Before Nate returned to Kerrigan's side, the few people who were standing in front of her had fairly quickly shaken Keith's hand and offered their sympathy prior to moving on. Kerrigan did not see or feel Nate walk up behind her. Her eyes were fixed on the casket, on Gail. She didn't notice Keith staring at her either. It was as if the room emptied out entirely and it was just her and the body of her best friend.

Did she look beautiful? No, she looked cold and stiff. And dead. Her face and her upper body, the only part of a body visible in a casket, looked much fuller. She never had the chance to work off her post-baby weight. And she would have lost every pound, every inch. Chances were lost to her for everything. To see her baby's face. To hold her. To love her and raise her.

Kerrigan walked closer. Gail was laid out in a red dress. A lady in red. A girl, a teenager, a woman who stopped traffic, stole the show, and stood out in a crowd her entire life. Suddenly, Kerrigan could see them as two eight-year-old little girls getting into Dottie Boyd's make-up. "You look stunning," Kerrigan remembered telling her, and she could still see the visual. The lipstick too thick on her lips, the mascara smudged underneath her eyes, and the blush overdone on her cheekbones. But, to Kerrigan, her friend hung the moon. She could do no wrong and never look anything less than beautiful. "So do you," Gail told her back then, and resumed looking at herself in the mirror.

She couldn't stop herself. Kerrigan reached out her hand and never noticed it shaking as she placed it on top of Gail's folded hands with a rosary intertwined. She never went to church a day in her life after she turned eighteen and her parents couldn't make her go anymore. Kerrigan was overwhelmed. Twenty-nine years old. A brand new mother. The one person, the only person, who Kerrigan used to be able to say she *loved her entire life*. The tears flooded her eyes and she tried to muffle her sobs. Keith, watching her, took one step toward her and then stopped as Nate wrapped his long arms around her shoulders, pulling her back and away from the casket, and she turned into his chest. Keith just stood there. Maybe he had to see that in order to know she no longer could be a part of his life, in any capacity.

Kerrigan quickly pulled herself together as a line began to form behind them. She turned to Keith and she opened her arms first. He then did the same as she walked toward him and they held each other close. More tears came from Kerrigan and she could hear Keith doing his best not to sob his eyes out, or his heart. Kerrigan was sure he already felt like his heart had been ripped out of his chest. He, again in his life, had been shown no mercy. He lost the mother of his child, just moments before their baby was born.

"I am so sorry, Keith," Kerrigan said, pulling apart from him as Nate remained at her side In her heels, Kerrigan now stood taller than Keith. And Nate towered the both of them. Keith looked up at him and Kerrigan immediately introduced them to each other. After a quick handshake, and Nate's offer of sympathy, Kerrigan spoke again. "You know how much I loved her. Despite everything." Keith nodded his head, and spoke softly to Kerrigan, "And I want you to know, she felt the same way." Nate still had his arm around Kerrigan's back and he tightened his hold on her as a way of letting her know he's there for her.

Kerrigan and Nate were going to step aside and allow Keith to take the time with the others in line, but then Keith spoke again. "I want you to meet her," he said, looking in the direction of the rows of chairs lined up in the middle of the funeral home. In the front, Kerrigan saw Keith's mother seated and holding a baby, swaddled in a pink blanket. Kerrigan glanced at the baby from where she stood and then looked back at Keith. She didn't know if she should do it, but at the moment she didn't feel like she had much choice. Nate waited for Kerrigan to make that move. "What's her name?" Kerrigan asked, trying to stall. Buy time. *I don't know if I can do this.*

"Abigail. After her mommy. Gail chose her name months ago. She wanted to call her Abby."

"It's a beautiful name," Kerrigan said, taking her first steps toward her former mother-in-law, and Nate followed.

She got close enough to greet a woman who had always been civil to her, but never very loving. "Hello, Carol."

Carol's eyes were teary as she remained seated, smiled, and nodded her head as Kerrigan looked down to see the baby. She looked like her mommy, and Kerrigan felt extreme relief. This baby did not have any obvious resemblance to Piper. Piper was an even mix of both Keith and Kerrigan. Abby looked solely like Gail. Kerrigan could handle these few minutes now. She took a deep breath, and Carol spoke to her. "This is just so awful. Keith finally has a baby of his own and his wife dies." Kerrigan had no idea they had gotten married, but she was not surprised. The surprise was how her former mother-in-law seemed to have forgotten how *she* lost Piper, too. *She* yearned for another baby, too. And *she* was Keith's wife first. Before Kerrigan could think of any response to such an ignorant statement, Carol spoke again. "You never should have left him. You two should have tried again for a baby. This could be your baby I'm holding." Nate could not take it anymore. He spoke up. "Ma'am, I think maybe you should stop talking. Sometimes, in grief, we say things we do not mean, things that do not make any damn sense." Carol looked at Nate and then back at Kerrigan, and this time Kerrigan had words for her.

"Take your sadness for Gail and your anger, or whatever it is you feel toward me, and turn those feelings into good. Draw strength from all of your emotions, because that baby girl you're holding in your arms is going to need you. Be good to her. Spoil her like Gail would have." And then Kerrigan turned and walked away.

There was no need to stay within those four walls of that god-awful room. It was the same funeral home she spent too much time in when her baby died. She wanted to leave.

"Where do you want to go?" Nate asked her as soon as he met her outside with their bags.

"Let's call that taxi back and go to the hotel," Kerrigan said, taking in the fresh air outside. She could not go back inside of that funeral home.

"What about the church service and the cemetery?" Nate asked her, knowing she could not handle being at the cemetery where Piper was buried.

"Gail hated church, so she'll understand… and I don't do cemeteries." Kerrigan tried to smile at Nate. Without him beside her right here and right now, she knew she would have fallen to pieces. Gail Boyd was dead. Keith had another baby, but he lost the love of his life. And her former mother-in-law was still a bitch. "And, I need a drink," she added with a smile.

***

They stayed overnight at the hotel, and only twenty-four hours in Baltimore. From her hotel room, Kerrigan sat on the end of the bed and called Keith. Nate had walked out of the room to go downstairs to the front desk to check them out early. Kerrigan was ready to go back home. To the beach. To their home.

Keith never answered his phone and Kerrigan didn't leave him a voice mail. She stood up from the hotel bed and heard a knock on the door. She thought it was Nate, returning without a key, but when she opened the door, she saw Keith.

"I just tried calling you," Kerrigan said.

"I know, I was on my way up in the elevator. Thought I would just talk to you in person. I saw Nate, he told me what room to find you in." Keith seemed more together today than yesterday, which was completely understandable. Kerrigan knew all too well what it felt like to be on the brink while standing in front of a casket in a funeral home.

"Come in," Kerrigan said to him and he walked in and closed the door behind him.

"Where's the baby?" she asked.

"With my parents. I had to meet with Gail's lawyer," Keith explained, and then he pulled out a white letter envelope from his back pocket and Kerrigan just looked at him. "As you know, Gail was a wealthy girl. She had her parents' money, assets and estate – as well as her share of the gym she owned."

"I hope she left it all to you and the baby," Kerrigan offered.

"She had her affairs in order," Keith replied. "I'm here to tell you that there was something left behind in one of her safe-deposit boxes at the bank. It was meant for you, but you never received it." Kerrigan looked confused. She wanted nothing from Gail.

"Whatever it is, Abby should have it. Give it to your daughter." Kerrigan was adamant.

"It's for you and it's not from Gail," Keith said. "It's from your parents."

"Jerry and Dottie Boyd?" Biologically those two were Gail's parents. Not hers.

"When they perished in that car accident, they did leave you something," Keith said, almost looking fearful. Afraid of Kerrigan's reaction. He could not believe Gail kept it from Kerrigan, for years. "There was fifty-thousand dollars, left in your name, from the Boyds. It was in their will for you to have it. Gail just never gave it to you." Keith felt angry. Gail had seen how they lived. Paycheck to paycheck. That kind of money could have been useful, and some of it saved, when they were married and struggling at times.

"Are you serious?" Kerrigan asked him. "Even after death, she continues to piss me off." Kerrigan actually giggled and Keith smiled at her. "Keep it," she said, "I don't want anything from them."

"No, Kerrie. Now is not the time to be stubborn and proud. Those people raised you and I know they loved you. You deserve to have what was meant for you." Keith knew Gail's share was far larger, but that didn't matter. He wanted Kerrigan to take the money meant for her.

Kerrigan reached for the envelope from his hand. "This would have come in handy a few years ago," she said, and he nodded his head in agreement.

"Use it to get started with your new life." It was difficult for him to see her with Nate. She looked happy. She really looked happy. Now he knew how Kerrigan felt when she looked at him and Gail, together. He missed Gail so much already. Kerrigan remained silent because she could read Keith's mind. "I am happy you found someone," Keith continued. "I hope he's good to you."

"He is," Kerrigan responded, realizing Nate was giving them some privacy. "It's not going to be easy for you, Keith, but I want you to have a good life. You have been blessed again with a baby. Hold tight to her, everyday. Love her like there is no tomorrow."

"You and I know best how quickly things can change," he added, and she walked toward him and fell into his arms. He held her and he cried. His tears were not for

Piper this time. This time they were for Gail, and one last time Kerrigan felt her heart fill up with love for her best friend. She had already grieved for Gail in so many ways. For a friendship lost. A sisterhood lost. And loyalty lost. Kerrigan didn't know how to feel now that Gail was truly gone. More than anything, she felt sad for Keith. And for their baby.

Chapter 27

It was an overcast day on the beach, and eighty degrees in the afternoon. The sun didn't have to be shining for Kerrigan and Nate today. All they needed was each other, a minister, and their little witness who also wanted to be called the flower girl.

Meggie stood in the middle of her daddy and Kerrigan because she said she couldn't pick a side. She loved them both.

As Kerrigan listened to the minister, she wished Hallie could be standing with them today. She felt a rain drop on the tip of her nose and she smiled as she wiped it off with her finger. Hallie was there. *Just don't soak me this time*, Kerrigan thought to herself as she looked up at Nate, standing before her, holding both of her hands. Their eyes were locked and their hearts felt joined as one when the minister pronounced them husband and wife. Nate bent down to pick up Meggie with one arm and they both kissed Kerrigan at the same time on each cheek. And then Meggie squealed, "We're married!"

In the sky directly over them, the sun instantaneously peeked through the clouds and a beautiful rainbow appeared. Kerrigan pointed out how it stretched across the sky above them and she told Nate and Meggie she was certain that was Hallie. It's her sign. She was there with them on their special day.

***

"I hope you will go easy on me if it takes me a couple of years to get our anniversary right," Nate said, bringing a bottle of wine and two glasses to bed. Kerrigan was already in their bed. It was their wedding night on the beach. Meggie had gone back to spend the night with her mother and Jenny. She voiced her disapproval about not getting to celebrate with them and they promised next week they would do something extra special with her. Like pizza and a movie.

"Why are you already concerned about forgetting our anniversary date?" Kerrigan asked him as he poured her a full glass of wine on the nightstand beside the bed and handed it to her.

"Because when you set a wedding date, a man memorizes that date, if he knows what's good for him," Nate explained. "But, here we are, four days later and I'm first now calling you my wife because you scared the life out of me when you left me at the altar."

"I did not leave you at the altar," Kerrigan corrected him. "Circumstances sent shock waves through me. And, please, never say anything about the life seeping out of you. I need you in my life now and for the rest of forever. Do you read me, Nate Stein?"

"Always, Mrs. Stein." Nate was now in between the sheets with his wife, sans clothing for both. He tried to take her glass of wine from her, but she balked as she took another long sip. He laughed at her before he said, "I would like to say something and I want you to hear me before you get too drunk."

"I'm not going to get drunk. I need to be coherent for my honeymoon," she giggled and finished the rest of the wine in her glass. As Nate took the empty glass from her, he set it on the nightstand on his side of the bed. Then, he turned to her, and spoke from his heart.

"Tragic circumstances brought you to this beach…and into my life," he said, as Kerrigan thought of her baby girl and the pain of losing her. That was a pain which continued to grow and worsen before it ever got easier. "I know life is hard and we may have some more craziness ahead, who knows. But, if we do, we will handle it together. Okay?" Kerrigan nodded her head. "Remember what I told you once before, we must savor every moment and not look too far ahead. Tomorrow is uncertain. We are going to savor what is happening here and now and leave the rest go." Nate pulled her body toward him underneath the sheets and he kissed her softly on the lips. "Now, let's review. What are we going to do for the rest of our lives together?"

"Savor," Kerrigan said as she kissed him long and hard, deeply and passionately. Beginning with kissing him, she certainly was going to savor every single moment.

Epilogue

Kerrigan jolted herself awake and immediately sat up in her bed. She felt like she had just fallen back to sleep. The baby was crying again. Nate stirred beside her. "Not again, geez, every two hours? That boy already eats like a man."

That boy, Hal Lee Stein, came into their world five weeks ago. He weighed almost ten pounds at birth and Kerrigan had fallen in love with him from the moment she gave him life. He looked just like his daddy, having short blonde hairs – like peach fuzz – all over his head.

As Kerrigan got out of bed, she didn't have to go far. Baby Hal's crib was in their bedroom and it was going to stay in there for many months. When she picked him up, snuggling her nose into his little neck, he immediately stopped crying. "I'm not so sure someone is hungry…I think he just wanted his mommy." Nate smiled at Kerrigan in their dim-lit bedroom. She was blessed again with a baby. Another chance to give birth and be a mother. Nate knew having this baby completed his wife. Her heart was now full. The pain of losing Piper would always remain, but Hal had already helped her, as no one else could, to heal.

It had been two years since they married, and their love and their commitment to each other continued to strengthen. Even through crazy times. Nate now has full custody of six-year-old Meggie. He fought to take her away from Bryn when the truth surfaced about Meggie's diabetes. It was a lie and a scheme which eventually failed for Bryn. She used their daughter and fabricated a story of her being sick to try to bring Nate back to her. Bryn never accepted Nate moving on with his life, and a new wife. She struggled with her sexuality, later revealing in therapy how she was never entirely sure she was indeed a lesbian. Shortly after Kerrigan became pregnant, through her and Nate's second attempt with in vitro fertilization, Bryn suffered a nervous breakdown. Meggie visits her mom and Jenny, regularly, but her home is on the beach with her dad, her stepmom, and her brand new baby brother.

Their family of four resides in the first of the three beach houses. Nate's house was the only one with two bedrooms. Construction plans were already in progress for when the baby needed a room of his own. An addition to the house was the only option, because both Nate and Kerrigan wanted the beach to be their home for a very long time.

MJ finally returned to live in her beach house, but after one year, she decided to chase another zealous dream. Nate described her as the stir crazy queen, as she could never stay in one place for very long. And Kerrigan called her a lifesaver. Without MJ, Orange Beach never would have been a place for Kerrigan to flee to, and a place where she could begin again.

After she rocked her baby back to sleep, she continued to hold him close as she walked through the house and into the living room. A lamp was still on by the couch and Kerrigan looked down at the photographs placed on the coffee table. She loved the one of Nate and herself with Meggie on their wedding day when the photographer positioned the lens perfectly to capture their smiling faces and the rainbow in the sky in the background. The black and white photograph of Hallie and her daughters always made her smile, with a twinge of sadness too. The newest picture was of Baby Hal, immediately after he was born. Kerrigan sat on the hospital bed, holding him, with both Nate and Meggie by her side.

And last, on that same table, a picture was displayed of a little blonde girl. Her smile, infectious. Her face and her eyes, so photogenic. Already at age two, she was her mother's daughter. Kerrigan only knew Keith and Gail's daughter through photographs. Every single photograph Keith had ever sent to Kerrigan had been a treasure to her. Sometimes it's just nice to know life goes on, for everyone, and there are ways to be happy and whole again.

Kerrigan held tight to her baby boy as she sat down on the couch and momentarily closed her eyes. A few seconds later, she opened them abruptly when the faint scent of cigarette smoke passed through the room. That familiar smell was gone before she could inhale it again.

"Thanks for everything, Hallie," Kerrigan said aloud as Hallie's namesake stirred in her arms.

About the Author

There was no specific moment when the idea to write Heartless popped into my mind and grew into a story that began with loss and unbearable sadness and grief. The story itself stems from life. We all have our trials, and hopefully the saying is true how *God does not give us more than we can handle*.

In my opinion, however, sometimes people are dealt hardship in excess and expected to deal with entirely too much. That is how the character of Kerrigan came to life. I wanted to write about a character where the reader is thinking, *Enough is enough! Help her to heal. Let her find happiness.* She did find happiness and that is the message in Heartless. To hang in there. To push forward. You never know what lies ahead.

Kerrigan's story begins with loss and she continued to lose. But, while she was struggling, she also was surviving. And that's when the unexpected gifts entered her life. Tragedy turned into triumph. Kerrigan gained strength from the people around her and eventually realized how we are placed on this earth for the sake of each other. We lift each other up. We pull each other through.

Tragedy happens every day in this world. Sometimes it hits close to home and forces us, reminds us, demands for us, to never take our loved ones and our own lives for granted. And most important, when pain and suffering enters our lives, we cannot let it overcome us for too long or it will end up defining us.

Thank you for reading!

love,

Lori Bell

Made in the USA
Charleston, SC
09 February 2015